She Lies

A Chief Inspector Cam Fergus
Mystery

Frances Powell

Other novels by Frances Powell

The Bodyguard

Mystery of White Horse Lake

Lady of the Wye

Ghost of Tara

A Ballysea Mystery Series:
    The O'Brien
    A Bad Wind Blowing
    The O'Brien: The Untold Story
    A Ballysea Christmas

Chief Inspector Cam Fergus Mystery Series
    Lady of the Wye
    Death in the Royal Forest of Dean
    River Wye Dead & Breakfast

Cover Design by Kim Bailey

ISBN 978-1-54398-774-4

Note to Readers: British spelling has been used in this novel.

Contents

Chapter 1

"Professor Henderson, over here!" shouted the young Associate Professor as he staggered back from the open trench where, minutes before, he had been carefully excavating what he presumed were ancient remains. Turning away from the horrific discovery, all of the colour drained from the young man's face as he suddenly turned, bent over, and retching lost the entire contents of his stomach.

Pushing himself up from his squatting position, at the far end of the dry moat below the outer Norman castle wall, Professor Henderson hurried to the group of students who stared, mouths agape, into the trench.

"What's so urgent, Jameson," the middle-aged, gray-haired professor asked as his eyes slowly followed the direction of the young man's trembling, pointed finger.

Taking just one look at their discovery, the older man turned away, reached into his pocket, pulled out his mobile, and dialed 999, "This is Professor Henderson, we're at Goodrich Castle conducting an archeological dig, and we've discovered some remains....No Sergeant, this isn't a 12th-century burial, not unless the people living then wore denim jeans. ...Yes, we'll wait."

Snapping shut his older model Motorola flip phone, Professor Henderson turned back to his students, "Nothing more you can do here team. Take a break and go on down to the welcome centre. When the police arrive, direct them up here. I'll wait with the remains."

As his students wandered down the gravel path towards the welcome centre, Professor Henderson climbed down into the ditch and being careful not to disturb anything, visually examined the remains. He was used to examining the skeletons of the long-dead to determine the cause of death, but in all his fifty years, this was the first time he'd been faced with anything like the remains that lay before him. It still wasn't difficult to determine how the young woman in the ditch died. Her skull had been caved in by a person or persons unknown. At least, the murderer was unknown for now.

Chapter 2

Chief Inspector Cam Fergus hated the return of autumn. The summer had been a warm and dry one, allowing Cam to spend his free time with his wife, Helen, working in their garden or enjoying the beauty of the area they now called home. Having been raised in Scotland by his widowed mother, they'd depended on the harvest from their gardens for the food on their table. The coming of autumn followed by the freeze of winter meant less food on the table for the growing lad. When his mother died the autumn of his seventeenth year, Cam, unable to find local employment, sold their small farm and moved south to London where he joined the Metropolitan Police. It was there he met Helen, and after thirty years and one particularly violent autumn, he agreed to take a position with the West Mercia Police in the Herefordshire market town of Ross-on-Wye. Walking up Church Street from his home overlooking the River Wye, Cam pondered why it seemed that autumn always put him in such a foul mood. He thought about the gardens growing barren, the leaves falling from the trees leaving their bare limbs stretching like skeletons into the grey sky, his mother's untimely death and the end of his career with the MET. To him, autumn signified in a word...death.

As Cam passed the centre of town, he greeted the early morning shoppers at the Thursday market and thought about how relatively crime-free the summer had been. Except for a minimal number of petty crimes, there hadn't been one major incident the entire summer. While most of the police work was handled out of Hereford, Cam had been able to convince his superiors that the town, with its recent population growth and the upswing in popularity as a tourist destination, could benefit from a small contingent of officers at the local station. It appeared that his recommendation for re-staffing the station on Old Maid's Walk had indeed proven to reduce crime.

Cam had just hung up his coat on the old, brass coat rack in his office, poured a cup of coffee, and switched on his desktop computer when the call came in. Taking the details of the reported incident, Sergeant Dan Roberts, slammed the phone down and raced to Cam's office. Dan and Cam had an excellent working, as well as a personal relationship. When news first came three years ago that the station was to be headed up by a former Met Inspector, the other officers were skeptical of the type of boss they were being strapped with. It only took a matter of days for everyone under his command to warm to Cam's no-nonsense attitude. It became apparent to all that Chief

Inspector Cam Fergus wasn't about to ask any of his officers to do anything that he wouldn't do. Cam, in turn, had come to rely on all his officers, but none more than Dan Roberts. As a local, born and raised in Ross-on-Wye, Dan was a valuable source of local knowledge and was more than happy to share this knowledge with Cam.

"Sir, that was the professor in charge of that university crew doing the archeological dig over at Goodrich Castle, they've found remains in the dry moat."

Raising an eyebrow as he lifted the steaming cup of coffee to his mouth and continuing to stare at his computer screen, Cam asked, "And why would he be calling us about some ancient bones?"

"Apparently, the remains are wearing denim jeans."

Jumping from his chair and nearly upsetting his coffee, Cam grabbed his coat, "OK, with me, Sergeant!"

Rushing down the hall, Cam yelled over his shoulder to the desk sergeant, "Call Mary and tell her to get up to Goodrich Castle right away, then get the SOCO from Hereford up there. We have a body." As

5

they headed out of town, Cam couldn't help but think to himself, 'another autumn…another death.'

Forensic pathologist Mary Hamilton was just finishing feeding her chickens on her smallholding in Lydbrook, just outside the Forest of Dean, when her work mobile rang. "Mary Hamilton. Yes, Sergeant…Goodrich Castle?… Ok, I'll get there as soon as I can…. Yes. Sergeant, I'm well aware that the Chief Inspector wants me there right away, but I don't think our remains are going to suffer if I'm a few minutes late; however, my animals might suffer if I leave them unfed and without water." Letting out a long exasperated sigh as the desk sergeant waffled on about the urgency of the situation, Mary continued, "Don't worry sergeant, I'll take full responsibility," before abruptly disconnecting the call. Mary Hamilton took her duties very seriously, but she also knew her commitment to living beings came first, and as a former small animal vet, she valued the well-being of her animals.

After feeding and watering the rest of her stock, Mary locked up her farmhouse and climbed into her ancient Land Rover, and headed down the bumpy, dirt track from her farm towards the B4229 for the ten-minute drive to the Castle. Arriving at the scene, Mary was waved through a barricade manned by a uniformed officer and parked the Land Rover beside the Crime Scene Investigation van on the welcome centre parking lot. The lot was the closest place to park for access to the castle. The rest of the journey had to be made on foot up a path that ran beside open fields on one side and wooded area on the opposite side. Mary quickly grabbed her examination kit, donned her overalls and stuffed some shoe protectors and gloves into her pockets. Mary always brought extras, because invariably, Cam never seemed to remember his.

By the time Mary arrived at the site, the weather had begun to turn as thick clouds darkened the sky, bringing with them a fine mist which clung to everything like a delicate spider web. Blue and white police tape cordoned off the scene, and the crime scene team was just finishing taking photographs and was spread out in the dry moat looking for possible clues. Chief Inspector Cam Fergus and Sergeant Roberts stood staring down into the moat at the shallow trench, as Mary approached, "Sorry I'm late. I was in the middle of feeding my animals."

Cam looked over at Mary as she handed him the blue shoe protectors and gloves, "No problem, Mary. I don't think our victim is going anywhere."

Grunting, Mary looked down at the body in the trench, the smell of now wet earth mixed with decaying flesh assailing her nostrils, "Well, let's have a look at her, so I can get her back to the lab, and determine the time and cause of death."

Before Mary had even put one foot on the ladder leading down to the moat, a gravelly voice declared, "Mary, I think you'll find that the young lady likely died of blunt force trauma to the head."

Whipping her head around, Mary looked up wide-eyed as she stepped back off the ladder and strode over to the man and warmly embraced him, "As I live and breathe, Jim Henderson! What are you doing here?"

Hugging Mary back, the Professor replied, "Its Professor Henderson now, and I'm down here with a bunch of my archeology students from Hereford doing a dig. I'm the one who called the police, but what's a veterinarian doing here at a crime scene?"

Smiling up into her old friend's warm brown eyes, Mary said, "Well, obviously it's been way too long. I had to give up my practice. It seems I developed severe allergies to my furry friends two years in, so I switched fields."

"And how's that big strapping Yorkshire lad you married?"

Cam's eyes flashed a warning to the stranger, but it was too late. As soon as the Professor realized he had misspoken, he immediately took Mary's hand and apologized, "I'm so sorry, Mary. I didn't know." Cam continued to watch the way the stranger looked at Mary and the detective in him quickly sussed that he may be sorry about saying what he did, but he certainly wasn't sorry that Mary was available.

As the rain began to pelt down, Mary quickly excused herself and climbed back on the ladder and slowly made her way down to join the rest of the team in the dry moat. Following swiftly behind Mary, Cam squatted down beside her in the now muddy trench, and asked, "What do you think, Mary?"

"The victim definitely has signs of blunt force trauma, but I'll need to examine the remains before I can be comfortable giving you a precise cause and time of death. As soon, as we can get her back to the lab, the sooner I can get to work."

Mary signaled for the team to bring a body bag and gurney to lift the remains from the excavation site. As they worked to remove the victim, Mary returned to talk to her old friend and calling Cam over, introduced the two men, "Cam, this is Professor Jim Henderson. Jim and I were at university together in Yorkshire. Jim, this is Chief Inspector Cam Fergus."

As the two men shook hands, Cam said, "Nice to meet you, Professor. We'll need to take a statement from you and your students. Since the area is closed off, I'm sure we'll be able to use the welcome centre to take the statements."

"That's fine, Chief Inspector, my students are all down there now. When will we be able to resume work on the dig?"

Shaking his head, "I'm afraid this is a crime scene, so for the time being the Castle and the surrounding area is off-limits to everyone."

"Chief Inspector, I think you and Mary need to see this," called Steve, the team lead, as they finished lifting the young woman's body from the trench.

Cam and Mary strode back and stared into the open trench. Under the decomposing body, and partially hidden by a layer of soil, was the skeleton of a second victim.

Shaking his head, Cam stared at Mary, "Are you thinking what I am, Mary?"

"If you're thinking that we have at least two victims of the same murderer, then you're right." Directing her attention to the crime scene team, she said, "Get photos and check the immediate area and then get both sets of remains back to the lab."

"We may have to bring in ground-penetrating radar to check the entire moat for any additional remains," said Mary as she followed the gurneys bearing the remains of the first victim down the path.

"Do you think that's absolutely necessary?" asked Professor Henderson as he followed Mary down the trail.

"It is. It'll save us from digging up the entire moat looking for any additional victims. It can be done quickly, and the sooner we are done, the sooner you can continue your work," replied Mary as she reached her car and removed her overalls and shoe protectors.

11

Cam had been following the conversation carefully, and reiterated, "As I told you before Professor, this is a crime scene, and the entire area is off-limits until further notice."

"That's unfortunate, but I suppose it can't be helped. As soon as you finish with my students, I'll take them back to Hereford, and then I'll come back and wait for your all clear."

As the two men walked into the welcome centre, Cam recalled how Mary's cheeks had taken on a rosy glow, and her eyes had lit up when she saw the Professor and wondered if there was something more in their past than just friendship. Cam made a mental note to ask Helen when he got home tonight. Helen and Mary had become best friends when Mary had stopped by with a welcome basket when they first moved to Ross, and if anyone knew about Mary's past loves, maybe Helen would.

Chapter 3

It took less than an hour to take statements from the students. There had only been three working in that trench, while the others were working in other areas of the dry moat. There really wasn't anything they could add to help Cam's investigation, but procedure was procedure and statements still had to be taken. The last person Cam interviewed was Professor Henderson, "Professor, you told Mary that cause of death was blunt force trauma. Did you examine the remains or touch anything near the remains?"

"No, I didn't disturb the remains. It was a visual examination. In my line of work, I've seen a lot of remains, but not in that state of decomposition. Bones are what I do, so to speak. But, I'll still be astonished if Mary finds a different cause of death."

"Thanks, Professor. If you leave your contact details with Sergeant Roberts, we'll notify you as soon as you and your team are allowed to continue with your research."

After the remains were transferred to the morgue for further examination, the police artist rendered a sketch of what the first victim may have looked like. The next morning, after Sergeant Dan Roberts finished checking the database for missing persons, and failed to find a match, Cam ordered a house-to-house inquiry in the village of Goodrich.

It was less than five miles from the station to the small village of Goodrich. Sergeant Roberts was very familiar with the village having taken his children to visit its Norman and medieval castle on many occasions. The small village of Goodrich had initially grown up around Goodrich Castle and had recently seen some new housing development. During the high tourist season, the relatively small population of less than a thousand swelled due to interest in the castle. Sergeant Roberts was glad that being off-season there would be less curious onlookers to interfere with the investigation as well as less an impact on the tourist trade for the castle and village.

The door-to-door in the village with the artist-rendered sketch of the victim was proving fruitless until he struck lucky at the small local pub. It was just a little past noon when Dan Roberts pushed open the heavy oak door and entered the small pub. As soon as his eyes adjusted to the dimly lit interior, he strode up to the bar. The occupants of the bar suddenly stopped talking, as all eyes followed the stranger. The pub was busy with what Dan suspected were locals, so he was hopeful that someone might recognize the young victim.

Sliding the photo across the bar to the barman, Dan identified himself, "Sergeant Roberts, West Mercia Police. Do you recognize this young lady?"

Pushing the photo back across the bar at Dan, the barman began polishing a row of pint glasses and turned his back, "Yeah, I recognize her."

"Are you sure this is the girl you saw?" asked Sergeant Roberts, pushing the photo back across the bar in front of the man who turned to face Dan as he continued polishing glasses.

Taking another quick glance, the bartender pushed the sketch back across the bar again, "I'm not likely to forget her."

"And why is that?" asked Roberts, growing annoyed with the man's surly attitude.

Slamming the glass he was polishing on the bar, "Would you be likely to forget someone who did over a thousand pounds worth of damage to your establishment and then did a runner? If you people would have done your job, maybe this girl would be in jail and not dead."

15

Raising his eyes, Sergeant Roberts starred deeply in the bartender's hooded eyes, "I don't believe I said anything about the young lady being dead."

"Look, officer, Goodrich is a small village, and this is its only pub. Anyone working at that dig up at the Castle stays at local B&B's and grabs their meals and drinks here. The body and the skeleton were all they talked about last week before they went back to Hereford. So, when you show up with this picture, it doesn't take a genius to make the connection."

"OK, so she wasn't a local and not one of the archeology team. Do you have any idea where she was staying and why she was here?"

"Nope, not a clue," grumbled the barman as he turned his back and walked to the end of the bar to wait on a shaggy-haired young man who had just entered the pub.

The pub was crowded, but everyone he spoke with turned away when presented with the drawing, denying knowledge of the girl pictured there. The atmosphere in the pub had grown decidedly cooler since Sergeant Roberts entered and began asking questions about the victim.

Finally, siding up next to the young man who appeared to be about the same age as the victim, Sergeant Roberts quickly identified himself and once again laid the sketch on the bar, "Do you happen to recognize this young lady."

Pushing his long hair away from his eyes, he smiled, "Yes, sir. I remember her. Her name is Ali. She was camping out over here with a group of people staying here for the music festival over in Ross. Is she in some kind of trouble again?"

"Again?"

"Yeah, she made quite a mess here in the pub. When she left, she even pushed over the phone box out front. I can tell you, she didn't make any friends among the locals."

"I see. Well, to answer your question, I'm afraid the young lady is dead. Do you happen to know her last name or where she was from? We've checked missing persons, and there's no one meeting her description reported missing."

"Well, you wouldn't find anything in your database. Ali was an American. She told me she was backpacking through the U.K. before going back to Uni.

I don't know her last name, but I do remember that she was a student at that real ritzy school in Boston where all those politicians go."

"Harvard?"

"Yeah, that's the one. Ali was studying law. I remember her spouting off about it after she caused the ruckus here."

"Seems strange that a girl studying to be a lawyer would commit criminal damage like she is alleged to have done," remarked Sergeant Roberts as he scribbled in his notepad.

"Well, she was off her face, wasn't she?"

"Drunk, huh?"

"No Sir, I would say something a lot stronger than that," said the young man casting his eyes to the floor and away from the glaring barman.

"I'll need your name and contact details in case we need to speak with you again."

"Tony Lambert, I live over in Lydbrook at Hillside Cottage."

Handing the young man his card, Dan said, "If you think of anything else, my direct number is on there. Give me a call.'

As Dan walked out into the bright sunshine, a shadowy figure sat in the far corner of the bar, staring down into his pint, and watching as Tony tucked the card into his jacket pocket.

Chapter 4

Cam had just switched off his computer and was getting ready to leave the station for the evening when his sergeant returned from Goodrich. After listening to Dan share the results of the house-to-house, Cam stood up and moved towards the office door, "It's late and tomorrow's another day. We should have the forensic report back from Mary tomorrow and hopefully, cause of death. Then we'll contact the American Embassy to see if they have anyone reported missing. You go home to your family and get some rest. It's been a long day."

Leaving his sergeant climbing into his patrol car, Cam waved goodbye and hurried down Church Street before slowing down to a stroll as he turned onto High Street. Cam smiled as he made the short walk home. He had never regretted moving to Ross. Cam was a country boy at heart and had never felt content in London. As he approached the house, he shared with his wife, Helen; Cam stood silently and deeply breathed in the crisp autumn air as he stared down at the River Wye. Although the house was way too big for just the two of them, Cam had been drawn to the house due to its location overlooking the river.

The sun had already set and Cam was so completely lost in thought that he didn't even notice that Helen had come out of the house and was sitting at the wrought iron table on their patio until she said, "Fancy a glass of wine before dinner?"

Cam jerked back to reality and shaking his head to clear his thoughts, "Yes, please, sounds like just what I need tonight."

"Another rough day?" asked Helen as she poured her husband a glass of wine

Taking the glass from his wife, "Yeah, we found out that the young girl is American and tomorrow it's likely that her parents will get the news that their daughter isn't coming home."

Helen reached over and took her husband's free hand. She knew that this was the part of the job that Cam dreaded the most. As the father of a grown son and daughter, Cam could understand the heartbreak that this news would cause. Patting Helen's hand, Cam raised his wine glass to his lips and after taking a drink said, "At least, this time I won't have to deliver the bad news. The American Embassy will have someone contact the dead girl's family."

Cam was silent for a moment as his eyes sought the moody waters of the River Wye flowing silently below his house before asking, "Has Mary ever mentioned to you a man named Jim Henderson who she knew from uni?"

"Jim Henderson? Let me think. Did he have something to do with ancient civilizations?"

"Yes, that would be the one," replied Cam tilting his head back to drain the last of the wine from his glass before passing it to Helen for a refill.

Refilling her husband's wine glass, Helen asked, "Why do you ask, Cam? Does he have something to do with this young girl's death?"

Shaking his head, "No, not directly. He's actually a Professor now, and he was heading up the team of students doing the dig at Goodrich who discovered the remains. He and Mary's warm reunion made me wonder if they had been closer than just friends."

"Oh, you think they were romantically involved, huh? Well, from what Mary has shared with me, she met the man she went on to marry during her first year at uni, and they were a couple throughout, marrying right after graduation. So, unless it was a brief affair before she met her future husband, it's highly unlikely. Brrrr…I'm getting cold, so I'm going in. Dinner in five minutes," replied Helen as she gathered up the now empty wine glasses and headed back inside to the warmth of her kitchen.

"I'll be right in," called Cam as he stood up and walked to the edge of his patio and stared across the river at the ruins of Wilton Castle which lay bathed in moonlight before muttering to himself, "I'll never get tired of this view."

Helen was just dishing up heaping bowls of steaming Cawl, one of her favorite stews from her childhood growing up in a coaling village in southern Wales when Cam hung up his coat and sat down at the table.

Sitting down opposite her husband she passed him the plate of homemade brown bread, and as they began to eat, Helen asked, "Why did you want to know about this professor and Mary, and what made you think that they may have been romantically involved?"

Putting his spoon down, "To make a long story short, he asked Mary about her husband, and when she told him that he had passed away, Henderson offered his condolences, but he wasn't unhappy about the news."

Helen laughed, "My goodness Cam, are you sure you're not overthinking this. It would certainly be a long time to carry a torch for someone if they haven't seen each other since university days."

Reaching for another thick slice of Helen's freshly baked bread, Cam winked at his wife, "I don't know about that, I've been carrying a torch for you since the day I first saw you in that second-hand book store by the Thames over thirty years ago. Mark my words; he has designs on our Mary."

Chapter 5

Mary was still working in her lab long after everyone else had gone home when the sound of a car door closing had her slipping off her examination gloves, and walking to the door. Looking out through the side window, she was surprised to see her old friend, Jim Henderson, approaching the door.

Unlocking the door and swinging it open wide, Mary smiled, "Jim, this is a surprise! I thought you'd be back in Hereford by now."

"Actually, I've been there, dropped the students off, switched vehicles, and returned. I told the Chief Inspector that I'd stay in the area and wait for his all-clear to resume the dig. I'm scheduled off for the next fortnight, so no sense in sitting around my flat doing nothing. I thought I could do a little more research about the Castle while I'm here, and maybe visit with my old friend a bit," he replied as he leaned forward and placed a kiss on Mary's cheek.

"Well, I was just finishing up for the evening and on my way home to feed my animals. Have you had your dinner, yet?"

"No, I came right here. I was hoping you might still be here, and I was actually going to ask you out for a meal."

"Well, give me a minute, and I'll finish closing up, and you can follow me to the farm. I live over in Lydbrook, but it's not far. Once I get the animals fed, we can get that dinner."

Mary smiled as she locked up the lab and joined Jim outside on the parking lot.

"I'll drive slowly, so we don't get separated. It's not very far to my place, but there are quite a few twists and turns," called Mary as she climbed behind the wheel of her old Land Rover and eased the vehicle out of the parking lot and onto the main road.

It was only a matter of twenty minutes before they arrived at Mary's smallholding. Climbing out of her car, Mary waited for her friend to catch up with her as she headed for the house. Holding the door open wide, Mary smiled as she ushered Jim into her kitchen, "Pull up a chair and have a seat. I'll run out and feed the animals. It shouldn't take long, and then we can be on our way."

"Can I be of any help, Mary?" asked Jim.

"No, just have a seat. If you fancy a drink, there's a small selection of liquor in the drinks cabinet in the lounge or beer and cider in the fridge. Just help yourself."

As Mary tended to her animals, Jim grabbed a beer and roamed around the lounge, stopping in front of a table laden with photographs, picking up a photo of Mary in her wedding gown; Jim smiled then muttered out loud, "Still as beautiful today as she was then. It could have been me. I was such a fool."

Mary stood silently in the doorway and overhearing her old friend's declaration, coughed to announce her arrival, "Just going to have a quick wash and change my clothes, and then we can be on our way."

Turning at the sound of Mary's voice, Jim smiled as Mary disappeared down the hall. True to her word, Mary was back and ready to leave in fifteen minutes. The drive into Ross was filled with talk of days gone by and remembrances of friends from days at university.

After settling for a dinner of lamb chops, talk quickly turned to the case. Between mouthfuls of fresh vegetables, Jim asked, "So what have your tests revealed so far?"

Laying her fork down as she reached for her glass of wine. Mary replied, "I'm not so sure this topic is conducive for enjoying one's dinner."

Laughing, Jim pressed on, "If it doesn't bother you, it certainly won't bother me. I dare say we've both seen enough dead bodies to become, how shall I say, somewhat detached."

"I'm afraid I've never been able to get to that point. I know a lot of my colleagues manage it, but I can't. That's why I never refer to the victim by their name. It's easier that way for me to disassociate myself with the person that they were, and the family and friends they left behind to grieve,"

Reaching over and covering her free hand with his, "Same Ol' Mary. You always were a soft-hearted woman. I guess that's why I was so shocked to find you doing this type of work. Come on Mary, flatter me at least tell me I had the cause of death correct."

"I've only had the victim a matter of hours, so it's too early to draw any conclusions. I will agree that the victim's head shows signs of blunt force trauma, but whether that was the cause of death or whether it happened post mortem hasn't been determined. Luckily, despite the damage done to victim one's face, the police have been lucky and found a witness who could identify her based on the police artist's sketch. Of course, all my findings will be submitted directly to Chief Inspector Fergus, and if he says it's ok, then I'll share them with you. Regulations must be followed, but I'm sure you understand."

Jim smiled and nodded his agreement before lowering his eyes to concentrate on the apple pie in front of him, but not before Mary glimpsed something strange in his eyes. Was it resentment or anger? As quick as it was there, it disappeared, leaving Mary to believe she had imagined it. The rest of the evening passed pleasantly with no more discussions about the case.

Chapter 6

Pulling off her examination gloves and stripping off the scrubs she wore when performing autopsies, Mary sank down in the chair and pressed the button on the recorder to playback the findings she had listed as she performed the procedure.

After listening to the recording, Mary picked up the phone and called Cam, "Hello Cam, Mary here.... I have the preliminary autopsy report for victim one. Time of death based on the rate of decomposition is within a week to 10 days. The body has bloated due to the buildup of gases in the abdominal cavity, and there is evidence of insects, namely maggots. One important thing to note is that there is evidence of pooling of blood in the front of the legs. Since the victim was found lying on her back, we can state with certainty that she was murdered elsewhere and left face down in that position for at least eight hours before being moved to the burial site. I'm still waiting on toxicology reports."

Frantically scribbling in his notebook, Cam said, "Excellent Mary. Is there anything else I should know?"

"As for victim two, I'm guessing that she's been dead about a year based on the soil and the weather conditions. It would take about that long for the body to be reduced to a skeleton."

"Is that all, Mary?"

"Not quite, and you better be sitting down for this bit of news. I had a DNA test run on both our victims, and they are sisters."

Letting out a low whistle, Cam exclaimed, "Bloody Hell, Mary! What's going on here? One sister killed and dumped in a grave, and a year later her sister murdered and dumped on top of her in the same grave. This is personal. We need to talk to the family."

"I don't envy you breaking that news to them. Bad enough to have lost one child, but two murdered and dumped like this. It's just inhuman. What kind of monster would do something like this to a family?"

"I don't know Mary, but when I first started working homicides, I promised myself that I would never rest until the victims had justice and the murderers were punished. I don't intend to stop now."

"I know you won't Cam. We should have the autopsy results on victim two in the next couple days and the toxicology report this week for victim one. I'm waiting for that before I give you cause of death. I'm not 100% sure the head injury was the cause of death."

"Good job, thanks Mary. I'll speak to you soon," said Cam as he put the phone back in the receiver and leaned back in his chair taking time to mull over Mary's findings before calling his team together.

After gathering his small team together, Cam began, "The autopsy revealed that victim one was murdered elsewhere and left lying face down for a minimum of eight hours before being moved. She was murdered between seven and ten days ago. Cause of death is still pending, but we still need to start trying to locate the murder scene. Now, our victim two was murdered at least a year ago. No definite cause of death, at the moment for either victim, but DNA reports indicate that the two victims were sisters."

You could have heard a pin drop as all the officer's stared at Cam in disbelief.

Chapter 7

Cam had arranged for a liaison officer to meet the parents of the victims when their morning flight arrived at Heathrow, and drive them to Ross. After allowing them the rest of the day to recover from the overnight flight, he and PC Anne Parks met with them at their hotel the next morning.

PC Anne Parks had joined the small contingent of police officers at the station on Old Maid's Walk during Cam's first murder investigation in Ross-on-Wye. She had proven her worth when she worked undercover to expose the murderer of members of a Shakespearean theatre group who had been performing in the grounds of Wilton Castle. Injured during the murderer's capture, she had since recovered and returned to work, continuing to serve the community.

Cam hated this part of the job. He had been glad when he had been spared the task of breaking the news to the parents that their child would never come home again when Ali Adams was identified as an American. While the American Embassy went to the home of Mr. and Mrs. Adams in Baltimore to notify them of the death of Ally, it now fell to Cam to break the news of the discovery of the remains of their other daughter.

Shifting uncomfortably in the chair opposite the grieving parents, Cam began, "Mr. and Mrs. Adams. I'm afraid I have some very bad news for you."

Obviously grieving and agitated, Mr. Adams leaned forward and said, "Yes, we know, the embassy personnel came to the house."

Shaking his head, Cam continued, "Yes sir, I understand, but I regret having to tell you that a second set of remains have been found in the same grave as Ali, and according to DNA results this victim is Ali's sister."

Mrs. Adams hand went to her mouth, as she stifled a scream, burst into tears, and buried her face in her husband's shoulder.

A very shaken, Mr. Adams asked, "Are you absolutely sure, Chief Inspector?"

"I'm afraid so, sir. DNA tests confirmed the relationship. Can you think of anyone who would want to harm your daughters?"

"No, they were both popular and didn't have any enemies, as far as we know. Our daughter Beth was a beautiful girl, but very headstrong. She would sneak out of the house and sometimes disappear for days. Then, one night after we argued with her for coming home drunk, she just disappeared. We didn't realize until the next morning that she had taken her passport and emptied her bank account. Because she wasn't a child anymore, the police waited 72 hours before doing any type of search. They were able to confirm that she had used her credit card to book a flight aboard British Airways from our local airport in Baltimore, the very night she walked out. By the next morning at 9am your time, she was in England."

"What brought your younger daughter to England, Mrs. Adams?"

"Ali loved to travel and traveled a lot. Ali was studying law and had decided to take off a semester to travel all over Europe before having to finish her last semester and sit for the Bar Exams. She usually used WhatsApp to chat with us. The last time we heard from her was fourteen days before we were notified of her death. When she failed to contact us after a week, we became concerned and reported her missing."

"Was she in England the last time that you spoke with her?"

"Yes, and that last call with her worried us, you see Beth was Ali's big sister, and while they were complete opposites, Ali worshipped her sister, and Beth was devoted to Ali. We are sure that although we didn't hear from Beth that Ali was in contact with her. The last time we talked to Ali, she said she had located a man who her sister had been involved with, and they had arranged to meet up. According to Ali, the man said that they had broken off their relationship after only a few dates and that Beth had moved on with her life. He offered to introduce her to some of Beth's friends and help her find out where Beth may have gone."

"Did she mention anything more about this man? His name, occupation, or where he lived?" asked Cam.

"No, she cut the call short because she said she had to get ready to go to the meeting."

"Do you recall anything else from any earlier calls that might help us?"

The couple looked at each other before Mr. Adams replied, "When you mentioned that you were meeting us in Ross-on-Wye, the name rang a bell, and I remembered Ali saying that she had been to some type of festival near here and that she had stayed in some forest at a hostel. She seemed very upbeat and said she had made a lot of friends here."

PC Parks stopped writing in her notebook, and looked at Cam, "Sir, there was an outdoor concert out on one of the farms not far from the Forest of Dean, and there are a few hostels in the area."

Looking back at the grieving parents, Cam nodded and said, "That's a start. We'll follow up on that first. We know she was in the area of Goodrich because she was thrown out of a pub after becoming drunk and causing a lot of damage."

Wide-eyed, both parents stared open-mouthed at Cam, before her father blurted out, "Something isn't right, Chief Inspector, Ali didn't drink."

Chapter 8

Sergeant Dan Roberts was leaning on his elbows sifting through the pages of interview notes taken by PC Parks of the meeting with the parents of the dead sisters when the shrilling of his desk phone caused him to jerk upright.

"West Mercia Police, yes this is Sergeant Roberts. What can I do for you, Mr. Lambert?

On the other end of the phone, Tony Lambert stood in the garden of his house, smoking a cigarette, and sweating profusely, "I remembered something about the last time I saw Ali. There was this man I saw her with."

"When can you come into the station and give us a statement, Mr. Lambert?"

"Not there, Sergeant. I don't want to be seen talking to the police. Ever since I spoke to you in the pub, I've had this feeling that I'm being watched. Can you meet me after dark, somewhere else?"

Looking down at his wristwatch, Dan asked, "What time and where?"

"At the castle at 7pm."

Dan made a note as he replied, "I'll be there," but the phone line had gone dead. Tony Lambert had hung up.

It was almost 7pm when Sergeant Roberts, pulled into the empty welcome centre carpark and taking his torch from the car, switched it on to light his way, and headed up the gravel path towards the castle.

It had rained earlier in the evening, and the moon had just come out from behind the clouds casting an eerie glow on the still wet castle walls. Having seen no sign of his informant, Dan started across the drawbridge that stretched over the moat when the beam of his torch rested on something on the bridge directly beneath the castle ramparts. It took just an instant for Dan's brain to register what his eyes were seeing as he quickly pulled out his phone and called for the emergency services, and then ran towards the body lying face down on the bridge.

Reaching down and placing his fingers on the victim's neck, Dan checked for a pulse. Finding none, he pulled his phone out again and called Cam, "Sir, I'm at the Goodrich Castle, and the young man that I was to meet is here, and he's dead."

Cam had just sat down to dinner and raised a fork full of meat pie to his mouth when he dropped the fork, "I'll be right there. Have you called emergency services?"

"Yes sir, as soon as I realized it was a body. I hadn't checked for a pulse at the time."

"OK, Dan. Cordon off the area, and I'll call Mary while I'm on my way."

Looking over at Helen as he jumped to his feet and grabbed his coat off the hook, Cam apologized, "Sorry Helen, there's been another death up at the castle. I have to go."

Going to the door with her husband, Helen gave him a quick hug, "I'll wait up. Call me when you're on your way home, and I'll heat dinner up. Oh, and if Mary hasn't eaten, bring her along. I have plenty."

Kissing his wife on the forehead, Cam was out the door and on the phone with Mary arranging for her to meet him at the scene, "Mary, its Cam here. We have another victim up at the castle. Sergeant Roberts is already there and has notified the team in Hereford and is securing the scene. I'm on my way now."

By the time Cam made the slightly longer drive from Ross, Mary was already there and sharing a cup of tea from her thermos with Dan as she waited for the crime investigation team from Hereford to arrive and take photographs before she examined the victim.

Within minutes of Cam's arrival, the Crime Investigation Team came hurrying up the gravel path and immediately went to work taking photos of the deceased. Pointing up to the castle rampart, Cam turned to Dan and leading the way said, "He must have fallen or been pushed from up there. Let's get up there and see what we can find."

As Cam and Dan made their way up the narrow, winding steps to the area above where the victim must have either fallen or been pushed, the crime scene photographers stepped back to allow Mary access to the victim. Turning the victim onto his back, Mary stepped back to let the photographers take additional photos before beginning her examination. Starting at the head, she worked her way down the young man's body. For such a chilly and rainy evening, Mary was surprised to find the young victim in short sleeves. Lifting his left arm, Mary called for another photograph before looking up towards the top of the rampart for Cam.

Soon as Cam's head appeared, Mary yelled, "The victim appears to have marks on his forearms, better check to see if you can find any sign of a struggle."

Waving his hand in acknowledgment, Cam and Dan began searching the area as Mary continued with her examination. Holding the victim's hand in hers, she called for another photograph and grabbing an evidence bag from her case, secured the victim's hands in plastic evidence bags.

"Cam, it appears there may be skin under his fingernails. I'll have to wait until I can get it back to the lab to see if it belongs to the murderer."

Cam's head popped up again, "No evidence of a struggle up here. Are you saying that this is definitely a murder?"

Rolling her eyes as she struggled up from a squatting position, Mary called back, "I'll bet my reputation on it. This poor lad fought for his life. He didn't step off that wall of his own accord. There's something else bothering me, Cam. I saw Tony earlier this evening, and he was wearing a denim jacket."

After clearing the rampart so the SOCO team could take their photos and conduct a further examination of the area, Cam quickly approached Mary as she stood gazing down at the young man's lifeless body.

Gazing into Mary's eyes, Cam reached over and rested his hand on his friend and colleague's shoulder, "Did you know the victim well, Mary?"

"I'm afraid so, Cam. He was a local lad. I've known him all his life."

Turning to the team, Mary said, "You can take him back to the lab now."

As soon as Cam and Dan rejoined Mary, Cam instructed his Sergeant to notify the victims next of kin before turning to Mary, "You're not going to do the postmortem tonight are you?"

"Goodness no, the poor lad can wait until the morning. I haven't had dinner yet."

Smiling now, Cam said, "Good, Helen told me to bring you home with me. She made meat pie and has plenty to go around."

"Oh, that sounds good. I've wanted to have a girl-to-girl chat with Helen anyhow."

As they walked down the path towards the carpark, Cam thought to himself, 'Now why do I have the feeling that Professor Henderson figures in this chat?'

Chapter 9

The light from the open door silhouetted Helen as she stood waiting to welcome home her husband and Helen.

"Dinner is ready. I hope you're both hungry," she called as she opened the door wide and hurried back into the kitchen. Giving Mary a warm hug before helping her out of her coat, Helen called to Cam, "Open a bottle of wine. I'm sure you both could use a drink."

"I can't speak for Cam, but I know I sure could. What in the world is going on around here? Three young people so brutally murdered and at Goodrich of all places. It's unbelievable! What kind of monster is roaming our streets?"

Helen felt a chill go up her spine hearing the normally stoic Mary speaking about the young victims with so much emotion, and wondered what had changed in Mary's life to cause this sudden personality change.

Placing steaming plates of beef and ale pie on the table, she took the bottle of wine from Cam and filled their glasses, before saying to Cam, "I take it from what Mary says that this victim was murdered, too."

Tucking into his dinner, Cam stopped eating long enough to reply, "According to Mary, the young lad struggled with his assailant before going over the castle rampart. Poor sod didn't stand a chance."

"What was he doing there at that time of night, anyway?" asked Helen as she raised her glass of wine to her lips.

Between bites, Cam said, "He phoned Sergeant Roberts earlier in the day, and asked him to meet him there. He said he had information about someone he remembered seeing with Ali Adams before she disappeared."

Contemplating the meeting place, Helen asked, "But why didn't he just come to the station to give his statement?"

Mary set her fork down and pickup up her wine glass, before saying, "From what Dan told me before Cam arrived, Tony said he had a feeling that someone was watching him, and he was afraid to be seen talking to the police."

"Tony? Did you know the victim, Mary?" asked Helen.

Furrowing her brow, Mary replied, "Tony lived in Lydbrook, not too far from me. I've known the family for donkey's years, and I've watched Tony grow up. He was a quiet lad. Never one to get in trouble, he seemed to prefer staying home, watching the telly, and playing video games."

"Oh Mary, I'm so sorry to hear this," said Helen as she reached across the table and patted her friend's free hand.

"That's the one major drawback of this job. I've lived in the area for such a long time that every time someone dies, or in this case, is murdered, it's almost certain that I will know the person. Normally, I can emotionally detach myself from a person's death, but when it's a young person, I really struggle."

Cam remained silent as he finished his dinner and drained the last drop of wine from his glass, content to listen to the two friends talk. Excusing himself from the table, "Ladies, I've got some phone calls I need to make, so I'll leave you two to catch up."

As soon as Cam had left the room, Mary asked Helen, "Did Cam happen to mention to you that the person who phoned in the discovery at the dig was an old friend of mine from uni?"

"Yes, as a matter of fact, he did. Cam mentioned he's a professor of archeology and that he had a group of his students there, and it was them who discovered the first victim. Cam felt bad about having to close down the dig and your friend having to leave and take his students back to Hereford."

Blushing, Mary replied, "That's just it, he did take his students back to Hereford, but then he came right back. He showed up at my lab, and invited me to dinner that very night."

Smiling now, Helen said, "That was nice. You did go, didn't you?"

"Yes, but we had to stop off at the farm first so I could feed the animals, and while I was doing that, I left him in the house. He didn't hear me come back in, and I saw him holding my wedding picture."

"Well, that's normal. People will always look at photos sitting around on tables. Is that what's upset you, Mary?"

"No, not him looking at it, what upset me was what I overheard him say out loud to himself."

"For goodness sakes, what did he say, Mary?"

Mary lowered her head before responding. "He said that I was as beautiful now as I was then, and it should have been him."

"Oh, I see. But why would that have upset you so much."

Standing up and facing her friend, Mary said, "For one, look at me. I know we're good friends, but I don't think even you, as kind as you are, could ever describe me as beautiful."

"Mary, beauty is in the eye of the beholder, and everyone's idea of beauty is different. To me, you are a beautiful person."

"OK, I'll give you that, but what about the other thing he said?"

Filling up their now empty wine glasses, Helen remarked, "I think we may need another one of these for this conversation. First, did you ever go out with this professor what's-his-name?"

Taking a gulp of wine, "His name is Jim Henderson and no, never. He was in our circle of friends, but more like on the outskirts, if you know what I mean. I remember him as a painfully thin, very studious, shy guy."

"Well, Mary that may explain it, perhaps he had feelings for you and was just too shy to approach you. Add that to the fact your late husband, who you were dating at the time, was a big, strapping lad, the poor guy probably felt he didn't stand a chance. I don't understand why what he said would upset you. Actually, I think it's kind of romantic to think that he's been carrying a torch for you all these years."

Cam entered the room before Mary could answer and asked, "What's this about a torch?"

Jumping up to clear the table, Helen said, "Just girl talk, nothing that you would find interesting."

Mary was on her feet, too and reaching for her coat, "I better be on my way home. I'll need to start early if we're to find out who murdered Tony."

After walking Mary to her car and saying goodnight, Cam came back into the kitchen where Helen sat finishing her wine, "Well Cam, your instincts were correct again. It seems this Professor Henderson does have designs on our Mary."

Chapter 10

Mary spent a restless night and was in her lab before the sun had come over the horizon. She was eager to get this autopsy over with as soon as possible. Three young people were dead, and Mary feared that a serial killer was in the area.

Suiting up, Mary removed the remains of Tony Lambert from the refrigerated unit and moved them to the centre of the examination room. Turning on her tape recorder, she slid the body bag from the gurney onto the autopsy table and began the procedure that she knew way too well.

"I am breaking the seals on the body bag. The victim is fully clothed. He is wearing denim jeans, no belt, a short sleeve shirt, trainers and no socks. There are bloodstains to his shirt, consistent with the head and facial injuries suffered from the fall."

Standing back from the table, Mary grabbed her camera and took another photo of the body, before proceeding. "The victim is a white male with shoulder-length brown hair and brown eyes. He is 21 years old and has the tattoo of a Welsh dragon on his left forearm."

Turning her attention to Tony's arms, she continues, "There appear to be signs of pinching or grabbing approximately six inches below the shoulder on each arm."

Turning off the recorder for a moment, Mary leaned over the body of the young lad she had watched grow up and asked, "What happened, Tony? Did someone grab you up there and where is your jacket, lad? It was a chilly night, and I saw you wearing it earlier. Did it come off in the struggle?"

She'd been working for three hours and had nearly finished the post mortem on young Mr. Lambert when the front door buzzer sounded. Peering out the window, she saw a local florist delivery truck and a man retrieving a massive bouquet of flowers from the back of the van.

Swinging the door open, Mary called to the driver, "Excuse me, I think you've made a mistake or have a wrong address. If those flowers are for the deceased, the bodies haven't been released for burial yet, and even if they were, you should be delivering the flowers to the church or the designated place of service."

Hustling up to the door, the bearded driver smiled as he pushed the flowers at Mary, "No mistake, luv.

The gentleman who ordered them was very specific about where I was to deliver them. There's a card if you don't believe me."

Snatching the card from the arrangement, Mary saw her name printed on the outside of the envelope, "I see. Sorry, I wasn't expecting them. Wait there, so I can get you a tip for your troubles."

Shaking his head, the driver replied, "Oh no, ma'am. That's already been taken care of by the gentleman. He specifically said that I wasn't to accept anything from the lady." With that, the driver winked, then turned and strutted back to his van, and was gone, leaving Mary staring down in astonishment at the flowers.

"Cheeky devil," muttered Mary as the driver drove off.

Carefully pulling the card from the envelope, she read its contents, *Thank you for a wonderful evening. Will you join me for dinner on Saturday night? James.*

Mary sat tapping the edge of the card on her office desk, and then reached for the telephone, "Hello Helen, its Mary. Are you free for a couple hours this afternoon? I thought we could grab some lunch, and then maybe you could help me with a little problem that I'm having."

"Of course Mary, is everything alright?" asked Helen.

"Yes, everything is fine, nothing to worry yourself about. I'd just like another woman's opinion on something. How about I pick you up at noon?"

"Sounds perfect, Mary. I'll be ready."

Hanging up the telephone, Mary stared at the large clock on the wall opposite her desk, just gone past 9:00, so still plenty of time to finish the postmortem and drop off the report to Cam at the station, before picking Helen up for lunch. Leaving the flowers sitting in the middle of her desk, she returned to her lab. The last thing that she needed to do was take any particulates from under the fingernails of the victim.

Removing the plastic evidence bag from Tony's hand, Mary gently held her young neighbor's hand in hers before saying, "Hope you scratched whoever did this to you real good." Scrapping the matter from under the nails, she prepared it to go for testing, hoping that a match could be found.

Chapter 11

Slipping out of her lab coat and running her fingers through her short hair, Mary grabbed the recently printed autopsy reports from the printer and stuffed them into the folder labeled Tony Lambert. Switching off the lights and locking the door behind her, Mary climbed into her Land Rover and drove the short distance to the police station on Old Maids Walk.

Cam was in the middle of his morning briefing when he looked up to see Mary standing in the doorway, "Come on in Mary, what have you got for us?"

"Not a whole lot at the moment. As I noted at the scene, the victim has bruising approximately six inches below his shoulders. From the bruising patterns, the markings indicate a grab, then what appears to be pinching."

"In your experience, Mary, what would have caused that type of bruising?" asked Cam as he took the envelope from Mary's outstretched hand.

"Like I told you before, Tony fought for his life. He didn't fall or throw himself off there. By the way, any news on his jacket yet?"

Sergeant Roberts spoke up, "I spoke with Tony's parents, and they confirmed what Mary said. Tony was definitely wearing the jacket when he left home the night he died."

Standing in front of the whiteboard that displayed a photograph of the deceased, Cam wrote 'jacket' and drew a big circle around it before turning to his team, "Why would the murderer take Tony's jacket?"

Dan Roberts theorized, "Trophy? Serial killers are known to take personal items of their victims."

"It's possible; however, there was residue under Tony's fingernails. I've taken samples from under his nails that appear to indicate that he probably scratched his attacker. The jacket may have come off in the scuffle, and that would explain the pinch-like bruises. If this scenario is correct, then in all likelihood, the jacket had the murderer's blood on it," said Mary.

"OK team, you heard what Mary said; we need to find this jacket. Check the area of the Castle, especially the wooded area next to the path, and along all the roads leading out of there. The murderer may have tossed It out of his car. Speaking of the murderer's car, any luck on that tyre tread impression?"

Dan turned and posted an enlarged photograph of the tire tread on the board, "Since the area had been closed to the public since the discovery of the bodies, we are confident that these tread marks are from the murderer's car. They appear to be made by a medium-sized passenger car with new tyres. So, either a new car or an older model fitted with new tyres."

Looking down at her watch, Mary grabbed Cam's arm, "Need to dash, I'm picking up your wife for lunch."

Walking Mary to the door of the station, Cam waved goodbye and immediately went to his office and not even bothering to sit down, picked up the phone, "Hello Sue, how are you?"

Sue and her husband had recently sold their home at Wilton Castle and moved south to be closer to family. Aside from being good friends with Cam and Helen, Sue had proven invaluable in Cam's more serious cases because of her experience as a criminal profiler.

Sue had just come back from her morning bike ride and was sitting at the kitchen table drinking a cup of tea when Cam called, "Hi Cam, I'm fine. How are you and Helen, and when are you two coming for a visit?"

"To tell you the truth, I would love to be there right now."

Sue could tell by the tone of Cam's voice that something was terribly wrong, "You sound upset, Cam, what's going on?"

"It's these murders of the two American sisters, Sue. The one witness we had was murdered the night he was to meet us with our first break in the case."

Putting down her teacup, Sue asked, "What murders, Cam? We just got back from a fortnight in Italy, and I haven't had time to catch up with local news."

Sitting down in his chair, Cam shared all the available details of the case with Sue. When he had finished, Sue asked, "How can I be of help, Cam?"

"I have no idea what kind of person we're looking for. I could sure use your profiling skills at the moment."

"I was planning on coming up your way on Saturday. I should be there between eight and nine, so tell Helen to have the kettle on."

"Thanks, Sue, I really appreciate it. We'll see you on Saturday morning."

"Don't mention it, Cam. See you then!"

Hanging up the phone, Cam hoped that Sue could give him some insight into the mind of a person who would murder one sister, and then a year later murder her younger sister and bury them in the same grave.

Meanwhile, across Ross, Mary was just picking up Helen for their lunch date. Having never dated anyone other than her late husband since they were students at university, Mary hoped to get some much-needed advice from Helen.

As soon as Helen heard the sound of tyres on her gravel drive, she slipped on her jacket and left the warmth of her kitchen, locking the door behind her.

Opening the car door and sliding in next to Mary, Helen shivered, "Goodness there's a chill in the air. How are you, Mary?"

Slowly backing out of the drive, Mary said, "Good as can be expected, I guess. I've been working since before dawn, so I'm hungry and to be perfectly honest, I needed to see a friendly face and not anyone connected with the case."

"I understand completely, Cam has been obsessing over the fact that they're no closer to solving these murders since day one. I can't even escape the topic at dinner time."

"Well, they'll be no discussions of that sort at lunch today. I have other things I need your help with," hinted Mary as she brought her car to a stop outside their favorite lunch spot.

"Oh, that sounds intriguing," replied Helen smiling widely as she climbed out of the car and headed for the café.

Both ladies settled for the lunch special of fish pie and were well into their meal when Mary brought up the subject of Professor Henderson. "You'll never guess what was delivered to me at the morgue this morning."

"Mary! I thought we weren't going to discuss the case," admonished Helen between bites.

"Oh no, it has nothing to do with the case."

"Thank goodness, I thought you were about to tell me another murder victim had been delivered."

Blushing now, Mary watched Helen's face for a reaction as she divulged her secret, "Flowers...Jim

Henderson sent me flowers to thank me for a lovely evening and wants me to have dinner with him Saturday night."

Helen lowered the fork that was halfway to her mouth before replying, "Well, that's nice, isn't it?"

"I don't know. The flowers were a lovely surprise, but I feel a bit strange. Jim's nice enough, but I really don't know him all that well and to be honest, I've never been on a real date since my husband, and I were courting."

Watching the concern cloud her friend's eyes, Helen asked, "Is there something else bothering you that you aren't saying?"

"Well, I was thinking about accepting his invitation, but I've already worn the only really nice outfit for our last dinner, and it's been a while since I bought anything new. I don't know anything about fashion or what's in style now. I was wondering if you could possibly go shopping with me and help me pick out something appropriate."

"Is that all? I'd love to go shopping with you, as a matter of fact, I need to pick up a new outfit for a wedding Cam and I was invited to next month. I can use your unbiased opinion on what looks nice."

Hesitating for just a moment, Mary confided, "There is something else? The last time we went to dinner, Jim wanted to discuss the case. I guess he's just curious because it was his team that discovered the body, but he seemed really annoyed when I told him that I really couldn't discuss the investigation. There was just something in his manner that disturbed me, but I could have just imagined it."

"I'm sure that he's just curious. I would be curious too if I were in his position, but I'm sure he respects your position."

Finishing their lunch, the two friends walked arm-in-arm from the café and headed for the shops on Broad Street.

Chapter 12

Helen heard the sound of tyres on her gravel drive as she put the kettle on Saturday morning. Peeping out the window, she was just in time to see Sue exiting her car and called to Cam, "Sue's here."

Throwing open the kitchen door, Helen wrapped her arms around her old friend in a warm embrace, "Come on in and have a seat, Sue. The kettle's on, and Cam will be right out."

Slipping out of her coat and hanging it on the peg by the door, Sue slid into a chair and accepted the cup of tea from Helen, "It's good to see you, Helen. How have you been? Any new gossip?"

Sitting opposite Sue, Helen smiled as she said, "I've been fine, and yes, there is a bit."

"Oh, do tell!"

"Well, I'm sure that Cam has told you about the discovery at the Castle by the archeology team from Hereford."

As Sue nodded and sipped her tea, Helen continued, "The professor who was in charge of the students just happened to be an old college acquaintance of Mary's, and it seems that he has taken quite an interest in her. As a matter of fact, they are going on their second date tonight."

Sue's eyebrows shot up, "My goodness, in all the years that I have known Mary, I have never known her to keep company with anyone. Knowing Mary, she must be all ins and outs when it comes to dating."

"You are right about that. We met for lunch, and Mary was asking me all kinds of questions. Then we went shopping so she could get a new outfit to wear. She wore her only other dress the first time they went to dinner."

Laughing now as she put her mug down on the table, Sue replied, "That sounds like our Mary."

"What sounds like our Mary?" asked Cam as he wandered into the kitchen and dropped into the chair next to Sue.

"I was just telling Sue about Mary's budding romance with the Professor," replied Helen as she slid a cup of tea across to her husband.

Rolling his eyes, Cam's only response was a grunt as he noisily stirred his tea.

Peering over her eyeglasses, perched low on her nose, Sue said, "Now, if I were a betting woman, I would bet that you aren't a fan of this professor."

Swallowing a gulp of tea, Cam was quick to reply, "As usual Sue, your intuition would be spot on. He's too self-important for my liking."

Receiving a disapproving look from his wife, Cam quickly changed the subject, "I appreciate you driving all the way up here to lend your expertise to the investigation, so I guess we should get over to the station and get started."

"Thanks for the tea, Helen. I'll stop by and see you before I head home."

Wiping her hands on the dishcloth, Helen walked to the door with Sue and asked, "You're not planning on driving home tonight, are you? Why not stay, have dinner with us, and stay the night?"

Smiling brightly, Sue gave Helen a hug, "That would be lovely. I was hoping you'd ask. I'll give Alan a call and tell him not to expect me tonight. See you later."

The station was deserted when Cam and Sue arrived, so after putting on a fresh pot of coffee, Cam led Sue to the briefing room. Perching on the top of the table closest to the whiteboard, Sue stared intently at the notes sprawled there.

"So, from forensics, it looks like almost a year between the two deaths. Did Mary establish murder as the cause of death in the older remains?"

"Yes, she found evidence that the hyoid bone was fractured indicating that the victim was strangled."

"And you said, the sisters' parents said that the younger sister traveled to England searching for her older sister."

"That's right Sue. The last time they spoke with her, she was going to meet someone that had information about her sister," said Cam as he filled two coffee mugs and passed one to Sue.

"So, either that person murdered her or whoever they told her about did."

Sue hesitated for a moment as she lifted the cup of coffee to her lips, "Cause of death for victim two?"

"Well, that's where it gets a bit strange. The toxicology report indicates that Ali died of a drug overdose."

Interrupting, Sue asked, "What's so unusual about that?"

"The victim also received a massive wound to the back of the skull, giving us the initial impression that she had died of blunt force trauma. During the postmortem, Mary determined that the injury occurred after she was already dead.

Cupping her chin in her hand, Sue thought for a moment before asking, "Have you discovered the place of death?"

"The only thing we can say for certain is that she was murdered somewhere else and left lying face down long enough for blood to pool in the front of her legs. When we found her, she was lying on her back, completely covering her sister's remains. We didn't realize that there was a second body in the grave until SOCO removed her for transport to the morgue."

"I'll need to see Mary's full report and photos from the crime scene, Cam."

Going into his office, Cam returned and laid the envelope on the desk in front of Sue. After a few minutes of staring at the photos, she said, "Notice how both victims are laid out, both on their back with their hands folded across their midsection? This wasn't a body dump; the murderer was careful how he buried them. He could have dumped victim two where she was murdered, but he chose to bring her here. In his mind, he felt like he was reuniting the two sisters."

"Any ideas where we go from here, Sue?"

"The key is the older sister. The younger sister was just collateral damage. She got too close to finding out what happened to her sister. Discover who she was meeting that last night, and you'll find your murderer."

"Any idea what kind of person are we looking for?"

"I'd say, you are looking for a local or someone very familiar with the area, strong enough to dig the grave and carry the bodies to the site. As I recall, there's no close vehicle access to the area, and then the murderer would have to get the bodies down into the moat."

"What's the possibility that the murderer had an accomplice?

"It's possible Cam, but I don't think so. I don't think the man you are looking for would trust anyone with his secret. I think that he is someone with a position he

74

needs to protect. Why else would he have chosen this site for the burials?"

"True, the dig at the castle was never publicized, so he probably assumed the bodies would never be found."

Sue grew pensive for a moment, "It's such a shame about Tony Lambert."

"Yes, he was our first real break in the case."

Sue's eyes grew moist as she replied, "I knew the family and watched Tony grow up. His parents must be devastated."

"I'm sorry, Sue. I didn't mean to sound cold-hearted. I have two sets of grieving parents and little information to go on, so the pressure's on."

"It's me that's sorry, Cam. I wish I could give you more to go on, but until we have more information, I'm afraid it's the best I can come up with."

Chapter 13

While Cam and Sue were going over all available evidence, PC Anne Parks was walking the streets of Hereford following up on the lead that the last call from Ali to her parents came from the town centre. It was an area frequented by students with many coffee shops and pubs. Armed with the new photo, pulled from the last image of Ali's video chat with her parents, she begins to make the rounds. After stopping in two coffee shops close to the uni, she gets lucky when the lady behind the counter recognizes Ali from the photos.

Leaning on the counter, she carefully examined the photo, "I haven't seen her for a couple weeks, but she came in here regularly for a week. She showed me a photo, too. Said she was looking for her sister and asked if I recognized her."

"And did you?"

"Aye, I did. The sister used to come in here almost every day with a young man. They seemed really cozy, if you know what I mean, until one morning they had a right Barney. She pitched her tea right in his lap, she did."

Taking out her notebook and taking notes, "Did you happen to hear what the argument was about?"

"Oh luv, what's it always about? He was probably seeing another woman behind her back."

"You don't happen to know this young man's name, do you?"

Shaking her head, "No, sorry."

Readying her pen, "Perhaps you could give me a description of him."

"Oh, I can do better than that. He's the one sitting over there," replied the woman as she pointed to a sullen-looking young man sitting alone in the booth by the window.

Moving in quickly, Anne called a quick thank you over her shoulder and approached the young man.

Holding up her ID, "PC Anne Parks, West Mercia Police."

"Yeah, what do you want?"

Positioning herself between the young man and the door, she slid the photos of the two sisters across the table in front of him, "I believe you were acquainted with these two young ladies."

"Yeah, what about it, I know a lot of young ladies."

"I'd like to ask you a few questions about your relationship with these ladies, starting with your name. Now we can do it here, or we can do it at the station."

Pushing up from the table and heading towards the door, "I ain't telling you nothing, copper."

Before he could even reach the door, his hands were wrenched behind his back as PC Parks placed him in cuffs, "Looks like it's back to the station then."

After advising him of his rights, Anne placed the still-unidentified man in her back seat and phoned Cam at the station, "Sir, I'm bringing in a young man for questioning. He admits being acquainted with both sisters but refuses to cooperate. He refuses to even give his name. He was identified as having an argument with Beth shortly before she disappeared."

Cam looked across the desk at Sue and winked, "Good job, Anne. We'll be waiting for you."

Putting the phone down, Cam smiled for the first time in days as he looked at Sue, "I think we may have just gotten our first break in the case. PC Parks is on her way back from Hereford with an uncooperative young man in custody who admits to knowing both sisters, and he was seen by a member of the public having an argument with Beth before she disappeared."

The fifteen-mile journey from Hereford to Ross-on-Wye took longer than the usual thirty minutes due to PC Parks having to pull over to deal with the combatant young man in her back seat. Foul language was one thing that Anne was able to ignore, but when her prisoner began kicking the back of her seat so hard that she could feel her steering wheel shake she'd had enough.

"Settle down, now! All you are doing is delaying us getting to the station. If you don't have anything to hide, then the sooner we can get there, the sooner you'll be on your way."

Anne's attempt at being polite was quickly met with another round of cursing and further kicking of her seat. Turning around and facing the road in front of her, "That's OK then. I have all the time in the world. We can sit here all day for all I care."

After a few more grunts from the backseat, the young man calmed down, and they were on their way again. Arriving at the station, Anne found Cam and Dan waiting on the steps.

"Is everything alright? We were just going to call you and see if you need assistance," said Dan as he approached the car.

"Everything is fine," replied Anne as she climbed out of the front seat and helped her prisoner from the back and into the station.

"Well, who have we here?" asked Cam as he followed Anne into the station.

Standing in front of the sergeant staffing the front desk, Anne shrugged her shoulders, "No idea, he refuses to give his name."

Removing the cuffs from the prisoner, Cam instructed him, "Empty your pockets and place the contents on the counter."

As the young man emptied his pockets, the desk sergeant began slipping them into an envelope, speaking aloud, "One set of keys, one wallet, and thirteen pounds in coins, Sir."

Before he could slip the wallet into the envelope, Cam stretched his hand forward, "I'll need to see that."

Flipping open the wallet, he looked at its contents and then at the prisoner, "Well, Mr. Charles Hopwood, we have a few questions for you, and the sooner you co-operate, the sooner you will be on your way. Is that understood?"

Head bowed, the now docile young man simply nodded before being led back to the interrogation room. Turning to his sergeant, Cam handed him the prisoner's ID, "Run him through the system and see if he has any other precious convictions."

Walking down the hall, Cam entered the interview room, sat down opposite the prisoner, and switched on the recorder, "Interview commenced at 14:25, for the record Chief Inspector Cam Fergus and PC Anne Parks attending. PC Parks will you caution the prisoner?"

Stepping closer to the table and addressing her prisoner, "You do not have to say anything. But it may harm your defence if you fail to mention when questioned anything you later rely on in court. Do you understand?"

Head down and staring at his folded hands on the table, the young man muttered, "Yes."

Sliding the picture of Ali across the table, Cam asked, "Can you tell us about the conversation you had with this young lady."

"Well, I was sitting in the coffee shop, and she came over and showed me a picture of her sister and asked if I had ever met her. She had been talking to the woman behind the counter, and she pointed me out as having known her sister."

"And did you?"

"Yeah, it was Beth. We went out for a while until she got tired of me."

Cam was just going to ask about the argument that was observed by the woman behind the counter when there was a knock on the door, followed by Sergeant Parker, "Sir, can I have a word? It's important."

Nodding in his direction, Cam rose to his feet, "Interview ended at 14:40" as he switched off the recorder."

Handing a sheet of paper to his boss, Dan Parker recited the information, "He's got a GBH on a former girlfriend, sir."

"Well, that doesn't sound good for him, does it?" remarked Cam as he turned and re-entered the interview room.

Switching the recorder back on, "Interview resumed at 14:42, so Mr. Hopwood, would you like to tell us everything you told Ali?"

"I told her that Beth and I had been going out last year and getting on fine, then one morning she walks in and tells me that it's over and she's found someone more in her league."

Cam looked puzzled, "league?"

"Yeah, you know someone who'd been to uni and had money like her."

Leaning forward across the desk, Cam voice remained calm as he asked, "So, if she was breaking up with you, then why did she poor a cup of hot tea in your lap."

"I called her a money-grubbing bitch, among other things."

"I bet you wanted to get even with her for that, didn't you? Like you got even with your last girlfriend that dumped you?"

Startled and jumping to his feet, Hopwood asked, "What's this all about? Has something happened to Beth?"

"Sit down. Yes, Beth's remains were found buried at Goodrich Castle. Have you ever been to Goodrich, Mr. Hopwood?

"No, I don't even know where that is. I'm from up north and have only been in Hereford for the last couple of years."

"When was the last time you saw Beth, Mr. Hopwood?"

"After the day that she dumped me, we never spoke. I did see her around town for a couple weeks, always with the uni crowd. Then I figured she went back home to the States."

Nodding, Cam asked, "And did you tell all this to Ali?"

"Yes, everything but the names I called her sister. She was really a nice girl, much different from her

85

sister. I told her about the last places I'd seen her sister and she left."

"Was that the last time you saw Ali? Is there anything else you can recall? You didn't happen to arrange for her to meet someone who knew her sister, did you?"

"Why aren't you asking Ali these questions?"

"I'm afraid we can't. Ali has been murdered, and her body dumped on top of her sister's remains."

Before Cam could even ask his next question, the young man gasped and began to sway in his chair. In an instance, Anne Parker was behind him supporting his body as he fainted dead away.

Opening the interview room door, Cam yelled down the hall, "Sergeant, call emergency services."

Chapter 14

Police procedure required that a physician be called if a prisoner suffered any type of medical emergency, so as Cam waited for the doctor to arrive, he re-joined Sue in his office. Sue had been watching and listening to the interview through the one-way mirror, and Cam was eager to get her professional observations.

"So, what do you think of our suspect, Sue?"

"Frankly Cam, I'm not convinced. I'm not sure he is capable of committing these murders or had the ways and means to do it."

Pacing back and forth and watching the hall for the arrival of emergency services, Cam finally perched on the edge of his desk and observed Sue as she began flipping through a stack of papers. Sue stopped and handed Cam the page she was seeking, "Appears your suspect is right-handed."

Cam thought for a moment before replying, "Yeah, why is that important?"

"According to Mary's autopsy diagrams and her notes, the person who strangled Beth was most likely a lefty."

Deeply exhaling, Cam stared into Sue's eyes, "Well, we can hold him for twenty-four hours without charging him. After that, we'll have to see if the magistrate agrees to grant us more time. The maximum they'll grant is ninety-six hours, after that if we don't have enough to charge him, then we'll have to release him."

Their conversation was interrupted by Sergeant Roberts as he poked his head in the office, "Sir, Hopwood keeps drifting in and out of consciousness, so the medical team wants to take him to casualty to be checked. Do you want Anne or me to accompany them?

"Anne can handle it. I need you here."

As soon as his sergeant returned to his office, after instructing PC Anne Parks to accompany the prisoner, Cam relayed Sue's observations to him, "Sue feels that it is unlikely that Hopwood is the murderer, so we need to follow-up on the one lead he gave us about seeing Beth hanging around with the Uni crowd. First, stop at the coffee shop where Anne apprehended Hopwood and get a statement from the lady behind the counter. See if she can verify that the prisoner has been in there regularly and see if she noticed anything suspicious when he was talking to Ali. Then fan out and show the victims' photos at some of the pubs nearer the university. Maybe someone will recognize one of the sisters. You can reach me on my mobile."

After Sergeant Roberts left, Cam picked up the phone and called Helen, "We're just finishing up here, what time is dinner?"

Helen balanced the phone receiver between her head and shoulder as she opened the oven door and slid the apple pie she'd just finished into the oven, "Dinner will be ready at seven. I just popped dessert in the oven."

"Great, gives us time to have a drink and relax before dinner, and Sue can tell us all about her new home."

The drive home only took a few minutes. Pulling into his drive, Cam and Sue climbed out of the car and headed towards the kitchen door. Before they went in, they stood quietly and gazed across the River Wye at Sue's former home on the other side.

Draping his arm around Sue's shoulders, he looked down at her, "You were here for so long, and you and Alan put so much of yourselves into the restoration that I'm sure you miss it."

Smiling up into her friend's concerned face, Sue hugged him as she replied, "Of course we do, at times. We have a lot of good memories there, but our work was done. The work we did has saved it for the future, and the new owners are lovely people. They'll take great care of the gardens we planted. All that being said we are thrilled with our new home and can't wait for you and Helen to come for a visit."

The kitchen door suddenly swung open, as Helen called out, "Would you like to take drinks on the patio or in the lounge by the fire?"

Pulling her gaze away from her former home, Sue called back, "A glass of wine in front of the fire sounds perfect," before turning and following Cam inside. The first thing that Cam noticed was still warm apple pie cooling on the wide windowsill, "That smells heavenly, Helen. Are we having custard with that?"

Helen looked at Sue and winked, "Some men never grow up, and when it comes to custard, Cam is still a little boy at heart. He loves his custard."

After a roast chicken dinner, Helen and Sue returned to the lounge while Cam pulled on his marigolds and filled the basin to begin washing up when his mobile shrilled loudly. Ripping off his rubber gloves, Cam grabbed the phone off the counter, "Fergus....Yes, Dan, what did you find out?"

Cam listened quietly before responding, "Good work, Dan. Call it a night and I'll meet you in the office in the morning, and we'll go from there."

Pulling back on his marigolds, Cam quickly finished the dishes and rejoined the ladies in the lounge. Pouring himself a glass of whiskey, he settled back in his favorite overstuffed chair and stared into the fire, deep in thought.

Seeing the worried look on her husband's face, Helen asked, "Is everything alright, Cam? I thought I heard your phone ring."

"Sorry, yes, everything is alright. That was Dan reporting in. He was up in Hereford, checking out our prisoner's alibi. It would appear that Sue's right. Seems that Hopwood is a regular at the coffee shop and lives close by. He is in there two or three times a day."

Sue was quick to note, "That in itself doesn't exclude him."

Shaking his head, Cam said, "Oh, there is more. The woman behind the counter not only remembered his argument with Beth but also his meeting with Ali."

Sue countered, "Well, we knew that."

"What she didn't tell Anne at the time was that a stranger followed Ali out of the coffee shop, and they walked down the street together."

"Well, that's a start!" exclaimed Sue.

Cam continued to stare into his glass of whiskey, "Well, not much of one. It seems that our mystery man came in with a group of students and went right to a table in the corner. One of the younger lads placed the order and picked it up, so she didn't really pay attention to him. Apparently, she was busy waiting on other customers, and when she looked up, she only caught the back of him as he walked out the door. That was when she saw him engage Ali in conversation, and they walked off together out of sight. All she could tell Dan was that he appeared to be older, and on the tall side, fit looking and dressed well, like a professional. She assumed it was one of the younger lad's father."

Thinking for a few minutes, Sue asked, "Did she recognize any of the lads?"

Shaking his head, "According to Dan, she assumed they were students because of their age, but this was the first time she had ever seen them in the coffee shop. So looks like another dead-end."

"Maybe not Cam, if you recall from my initial assessment, the murderer is most likely an older, professional man. His physical description would match with my profile, and if he is fit like she says, then he could have managed the movement of the bodies."

While Sue and Cam discussed the case, Helen had excused herself to go make the custard for the apple pie. Emerging from the kitchen, she asked, "Anyone want coffee with their pie?"

With everyone now gathered around the kitchen table and tucking into Helen's delicious pie and drinking coffee, the conversation about the case was soon replaced by local news. Sue and Alan had missed the carnival this year for the first time in years, so Sue was eager to hear about all the events, as well as the proposed sale of the town's landmark hotel. Finally, before heading for bed, the conversation turned to Mary, as everyone wondered how her date had gone that night.

Chapter 15

Mary opened one eye and groaned loudly. Her head was throbbing like a brass band rehearsing for a parade had taken up residence right between her eyes. Flopping back onto the mattress after unsuccessfully trying to push herself up on my elbow, she muttered out loud, "What the hell? I didn't drink that much Champagne last night."

After three more attempts, Mary finally sat up and eased herself over to the side of the bed. It was then she noticed. Looking down, she suddenly realized she was stark naked. Squinting, she looked around her usually tidy bedroom. The new outfit she had worn to her dinner date the night before lay strewed all over the bedroom floor. Wrapping her coverlet around her, Mary reached for the blouse that lay closest to her feet and held it up. It was torn all the way down the front, and all of its buttons were missing.

Sitting back on the edge of her bed, Mary tried to concentrate and remember what had happened last night, and how she had ended up naked in bed. No matter how hard she tried, she couldn't remember anything. Shuffling over to the window, Mary pulled the curtains aside and peered out into the courtyard. Her

Land Rover was parked there in its usual spot, but there was no sign of the Professor's car. He was gone.

With the throbbing in her head growing in intensity, Mary grabbed her robe off the hook on the back of her bedroom door and made her way into the kitchen. Switching on the kettle, she rummaged in the cabinet above the sink until her fingers closed around a bottle of Paracetamol. Opening the lid, she dropped two pills out into her hand as she spooned copious amounts of sugar into her mug of tea.

Taking the pills as she slowly sipped her sweet tea, Mary sat quietly trying to remember anything at all after dessert at the restaurant. She could remember their arrival at the Forge and her dinner of roast lamb with all the fixings. She remembered drinking three glasses of champagne with the meal and then going to the Ladies while Jim ordered dessert and coffee, but after her Eton Mess…nothing.

A sudden scratching at her kitchen door startled Mary, causing her hand to shake, sending tea down the front of her robe and onto the floor. Hurrying to the door, she flung it open to find Jess, her sheepdog, standing there, soaking wet. Grabbing a towel, she began to quickly dry him as she soothed him, "What happened fellow, I'm so sorry. I would never have left you out all night."

As she quickly filled Jess's bowl with food and water, she thought, 'He must have locked him out last night.' Once Jess had settled down and curled up on his bed by the kitchen range, Mary headed for the shower.

After staying in the hot shower until the room was so steamed up she could barely see her hand in front of her face, Mary quickly dried herself off, dressed, and went out to feed her animals. As she scattered the chicken feed in the courtyard, she tried to recall everything that she could about dinner before everything went blank. Mary wondered if she had in her innocence missed some sexual innuendo. Had she said or done anything that might have led Jim to believe that she was up for a shag or had he just brought her home, and she undressed and got into bed without bothering to put her nightdress on?

Once the animals were taken care of, Mary locked up her house, climbed in her Range Rover, and headed to her office. The toxicology reports from Ali and DNA results for the residue under Tony's fingernails were due today, and she wanted to get the results to Cam as soon as possible. Mary had every intention of going straight to work, but when she spied Helen out on her patio, watering her potted plants, she pulled into her drive. As soon as Helen spotted her friend, she broke into a broad smile and approached the car, "How was your date?" One look at Mary's face told her she had asked the wrong question, as Mary's eyes welled up with tears, and she covered her face with her hands. Helping Mary from the car and into the house, she sat her down at the table, switched on the kettle and pulled her chair up close to her friend's, "Mary, what in the world happened? Did you and Jim have an argument?"

By now, Mary was sobbing so hard, all she could do was shake her head. Getting up to grab a handkerchief for her friend, Helen quickly fixed the tea and placing an arm around Mary's shoulders, "You just sit quietly now and have your tea, we can talk about it when you're ready. I have all day."

Helen knew that whatever it was must have been traumatic for Mary to break down like this. The only time she had seen Mary cry was when a young person she had known all their life died tragically. Helen quickly fixed her own cup of tea and quickly re-joined Mary at the table. Mary's usually steady hand was shaking as she lifted the teacup to her lips, "I don't know quite how to say this."

Helen reached over and placed her hand over her friend's free hand, "It's been my experience that it's best to just blurt it out."

With that, Mary did just that, "I woke up naked in bed this morning with my clothes scattered all around my bedroom."

Helen's eyes widened, and she hesitated before saying, "I take it by your reaction that you aren't exactly happy about that. What did Jim say?"

Shaking her head, Mary said, "Jim wasn't there. I was alone, and the truth be told, I don't remember how I even got home or into my bed."

"My goodness, Mary. Did you have too much to drink?"

"That's just it, I didn't. I think someone must have put something in my drink," whispered Mary, her voice cracking with emotion.

Helen could feel herself growing very angry but trying to remain calm, asked, "By someone, you mean Professor Henderson?"

Covering her face with her hands, Mary sobbed, "Yes, he must have put something in my coffee when I went to the Ladies."

Jumping up from the table, Helen grabbed the phone, "I'm calling Cam."

Before Helen could even dial the number, she heard the sound of tyres on the gravel drive. Looking out the window, she saw Cam approaching clasping what looked like an evidence bag in his hand.

Walking into the kitchen, Cam held up the bag to Helen, "A member of the search team found Tony's jacket. I was just on the way to drop it off to Mary when I spotted her car here. Mary, sorry I called you last night and interrupted your dinner date. I meant to drop it off at your office last night, as I promised, but I figured it could wait until this morning. "

It only took one look at his wife's face for Cam to realize something terrible had happened, "Helen? Mary? What's happened?"

Cam sat down opposite Mary and waited patiently for her to compose herself enough to repeat what she had just told Helen. Once she had finished, Cam asked, "What is the last thing you can remember?"

Leaning forward on the table and resting her head in her hands, Mary thought for a minute before replying, "I remember taking your call and Jim asking me if it was something that I needed to attend to immediately. I told him that the search team had finally located young Tony's missing jacket and I was hoping to be able to use it to help identify who had pushed him off the castle turret. But it could wait until tomorrow since you were going to drop it off at the lab."

"Then what happened, Mary?"

"Well, we had just finished our meal, and Jim ordered dessert and coffee while I went to the Ladies. I can vaguely recall eating my dessert and Jim helping me to the car but after that...nothing."

"Did you have too much to drink?"

Shaking her head, "I can hold my liquor, Cam. I think someone put something in my coffee."

Cam's hand involuntarily formed a fist as he asked, "And by someone, you mean Professor Henderson?"

Mary stared into Cam's eyes and just nodded her agreement.

"Well, I don't need to tell you this Mary, but there's only one sure way to tell if you've been drugged. Let's get you over to the lab and get one of your assistants to draw some blood. We don't want to accuse an old friend of this if we aren't sure, now do we? You're too upset to be driving, so leave your car here, and I'll bring you back here when you finish up at the lab."

Mary nodded her agreement and followed Cam to his car for the short drive to the lab.

Chapter 16

Sergeant Dan Roberts had spent the best part of the evening and following morning visiting the coffee shops and pubs closest to the university. While he was verifying Hopwood's alibi with the counter lady at the coffee shop, an elderly lady with purple-tinted hair approached him.

"Excuse me, I couldn't help but hear you asking about Charlie and that pretty little American girl he was talking to a few weeks back. See, I was sitting at the next table, and I heard their entire conversation."

"Yes ma'am, Mr. Hopwood has told us about talking to her."

"I know it's not nice to eavesdrop, but I wasn't the only one listening to their conversation," she continued as her wrinkled face turned to stare off to a nearly hidden table in the corner.

Before Sergeant Roberts could interrupt her, she continued, "I saw him watching her, and he followed her out the door and was talking to her, then they walked down the pavement together."

Taking his notepad out, he ushered the elderly lady to the closest table, held out a chair for her, then sitting opposite her, pulled out his notebook, "Ma'am, I'm Sergeant Dan Roberts of West Mercia Police, could you give us your name and address?"

"Miss Alma Lacey, 61 Cottage Lane. I come in here every day for my morning tea and a teacake after I finish my morning shopping, so I know everyone who comes in here regularly."

"So had you seen this man in here before?"

"Yes, he has been in here a number of times, usually with some younger people. Students, I expect."

Scribbling into his notepad, Dan asked, "Can you describe this man you saw talking to the young lady?"

Tutting, the elderly lady said, "Of course I can, I might be old, but I have perfect vision, and my memory hasn't failed me. He was older, I would say early 50's, and about your height, 13 stone, brown hair with grey at the temples, high forehead, dressed in a tweed sport coat...brown it was, and oh yes, denim jeans."

"Well, that's quite a detailed description, Miss Lacey. Is there anything else?"

Thinking for a minute, the old lady replied, "Yes, I noticed when he was drinking his coffee...he's left-handed."

Dan smiled at the elderly lady, and handed her his card, "If you think of anything else, please call me. You have been very helpful."

With that, Miss Lacey stood up and grabbing her bag of groceries, waved goodbye and headed out the door, leaving Dan shaking his head as he returned to speak to the lady working the counter, "She missed her calling, she would have been a good detective."

Laughing, the woman said, "Didn't she tell you?"

"Tell me what?" asked Dan.

"Our Miss Lacey is the former Detective Chief Inspector Lacey with the London Met. She retired after thirty years of service."

Dan walked to the door and watched the little old lady cross the street and smiled, "Well, I'll be jiggered."

Thanking the counter lady, Dan walked out the door and headed towards his car, reaching for his mobile he called Cam, "Sir, I've just verified Mr. Hopwood's alibi and while I was there I had a conversation with an elderly lady that gave me a detailed description of the mystery man that Hopwood told us about. The funny thing was that it appears the old lady was a Detective Chief Inspector at the Met before retiring."

Cam was just preparing to drive Helen to the lab, when he stopped and asked, "What was her name, Dan?"

"Miss Alma Lacey," replied Dan.

"You're kidding? Well, I'll be damned. She was one of the finest DCI's that the Met ever turned out. Did you get her address?"

"Yes, Sir, I have it right here."

"Alright, I'm heading over to the lab with Mary. You go over and see Miss Lacey and ask if she could spare some time to come in and work with the police artist to see if we can put a face to this mystery man. Tell her that I have personally requested her assistance. She'll remember me. I'll call the station and have PC Parks process Mr. Hopwood for release and arrange his escort back to Hereford."

Chapter 17

As soon as Cam pulled his car to a stop in front of the low, brick building that served as the morgue and Mary's lab, he realized that something was wrong. Lucy Martin, Mary's young assistant, was pacing up and down, clutching her mobile phone in her hand and shouting into it. As soon as she spotted Cam, she ran over to his car, "Well, you really got here fast!"

Exiting the car, Mary ran to her assistant, "What in the world is wrong, Lucy?"

Grabbing Mary by the forearms, she exclaimed, "Someone's broken into the offices and trashed everything!"

Cam quickly placed a call for the Crime Scene Investigation team, and waited while Mary calmed down her assistant before asking, "Do you have any gloves in your pockets, Mary?"

Mary always carried extra crime scene examination gloves in her over-sized coat pockets, knowing full well that Cam always forgot his. In all the time that they had worked together, Cam never remembered to bring his own. After instructing Lucy to sit and wait in Cam's car, Mary handed Cam a pair of gloves, and the two of them entered the lab.

Lucy hadn't exaggerated as Cam and Mary made their way into the offices they found filing cabinets and desk drawers pulled open, and their contents spread all over the floor. Leaving Cam to look around the office for clues, Mary quickly made her way down the hall to the autopsy room. Pushing open the metal doors, she breathed a sigh of relief, "Thank goodness, nothing seems to be disturbed in here," she called to Cam.

Wandering down the hall, Cam placed his hand on Mary's shoulder and asked, "Didn't you have a television and video recorder in your office?"

"Yes, we just bought them. I guess they're gone, huh?"

"They sure are. It looks like a typical break-in, probably kids or someone with a drug habit looking for something easy to sell. We'll have the team dust for prints, of course, and then you and Lucy can try to get everything put back where it belongs. Let me know if you do find that anything else is missing."

Cam and Mary had just walked outside when the Crime Team pulled into the drive, followed by Jim

Henderson. Pulling his car to a stop behind the police van, he jumped out and ran over to Mary, "Mary, I went to the farm as soon as I woke up, but you had already left. I was just coming to see you. Are you alright? What's happened here?"

Before Mary had a chance to utter a reply, Cam took Henderson by the arm and walked him back towards his car, "There's been a break-in here at the lab. I'm sure you'll understand when I tell you that this is a crime scene, so we can't have you, or any other member of the public trampling all over the scene."

Nodding his head, Henderson lowered his voice, "I understand Chief Inspector, but I was extremely concerned about Mary this morning, and just had to find her and see if she was alright after last night."

Acting the innocent, Cam asked, "Why? What happened last night that would cause you to be so worried about Mary?"

"I'm afraid it was entirely my fault. I should have realized Mary was a bit nervous about dating after all these years and wasn't used to Champagne. I'm afraid she drank way too much. I almost had to carry her to my car, and when we got to her farm, I tried to help her get undressed and into bed and she... well..."

"She…well…what ?"

Henderson's voice dropped to a whisper, as he leaned closer to Cam's face, "She must have thought I was getting amorous and literally ripped her blouse off. Under normal conditions, I would have been more than happy about the prospect, but I have way too much baggage in my life, besides I am not the type of man that would take advantage of any woman in that state. I managed to disengage myself and left. When I woke up this morning, I was worried. The last thing I want is for Mary to feel embarrassed, so please don't mention any of this to her. "

Cam's eyes searched Henderson's face. He didn't like the man and was almost sorry that he had reopened the archeological site to the students last week, giving him an excuse to hang around, but something about his demeanor left Cam wondering if he had misjudged the man. Until he could determine whether he was telling the truth or a con man, Cam wasn't going to do anything to cause Mary any further distress. Finally, Cam took Henderson by the elbow, and maneuvered him back to his car, "Mary has had enough upset for this morning with the break-in, and is going to be very busy the rest of the day. I think it would be a good idea to wait until tomorrow to talk to her."

Climbing into his car, Henderson hung out the window as he started to reverse his car out of the parking lot, "Whatever you say, Chief Inspector. I don't want to cause her any further distress. I'll be back working at the dig with my students for the rest of the week before we head back to Hereford."

Cam nodded and turned on his heel and headed back into the lab. Reaching the door, he turned and stared at the retreating tail lights of the Professor's car before muttering, "Baggage…what baggage?"

Pulling out his mobile, Cam quickly called Sergeant Roberts, "Dan, Cam here. I just had a conversation with Professor Henderson, and he mentioned having a lot of what he referred to as 'baggage' in his life. Run a full background on him. I want to know everything there is about him. Yes, full financials, too."

On the other end of the line, Dan said, "Sir, I spoke to Miss Lacey, and she can come in after the weekend. She has family members coming for a long-awaited visit and didn't want to put them off until another time."

"That's fine, Dan. At her age, her family is the most important thing to her. Just make sure that the police artist is available when Miss Lacey can come, and Dan, you pick her up and see she gets home safely."

"Yes Sir," replied Dan as he hung up the phone and headed back to his office to begin the background check on Professor Jim Henderson.

Slipping his phone back into his pocket, Cam entered the lab to find Mary sitting on the floor gathering up the envelopes scattered about. Looking up at the sound of his approaching footsteps, "Well, I called the lab in Hereford, and those DNA tests on the scrapping from under Tony's nails were delivered last night, and from what I've been able to determine so far, they're missing. I hate to say this, but I have a horrible feeling that Jim has something to do with this. How could I be so stupid as to think a man like him would be interested in me?"

Squatting down beside his friend, Cam consoled her, "Slow down, Mary. It's not like you to jump to conclusions like this."

"Well, what should I think, Cam? Other than you and me, he was the only one I told that I was expecting the results of the tests to be delivered late yesterday. Add that to the fact that he obviously drugged me last night, and I think my conclusions hold a lot of merits."

Cam debated for a few moments before deciding to tell Mary about his conversation with the Professor, "I see your point, Mary, but isn't it possible that just perhaps you did have too much Champaign last night, and that he was only trying to get you home and into bed."

Growing angry, Mary exclaimed, "Yeah, he wanted to get me into bed, alright!"

"Calm down, Mary. Now, is there any other possible explanation for what happened when you got home?"

Mary sat cross-legged on the floor, not saying a word, until suddenly her face turned blood red, "Oh dear lord, Cam, I remember now. It must have been the drink. I'm only used to drinking ciders and beers, and I'd eaten nothing before the first two glasses. I've made a terrible fool of myself. What must Jim think?"

"Well, I can tell you this much, Mary, Professor Henderson was very concerned about you, and that was why he came here this morning. He said under normal conditions, he would have been pleased with your invitation; however, he said that he wasn't the type of man to take advantage and that he had too much 'baggage.' Do you know what he means by that?"

Wrinkling her brow, Mary slowly shook her head, "No, I have no idea, Cam. I hadn't seen or heard from Jim since we were at uni together. I don't know anything about his personal life between then and now. You don't suppose he has a wife somewhere, do you Cam?"

"I've no idea, Mary, but I've asked Dan to run a complete background check on him. We should know later today."

"And I should have a copy of the DNA report by then too. Maybe, we'll get lucky, and our murderer will be in the database."

Standing up and reaching a hand down to Mary, Cam helped her to her feet, "Well, it looks like you'll be tied up here for a while. How about I swing by here and pick you up for lunch?"

Shaking her head, "I'm not really hungry, Cam."

"Nonsense, I bet you didn't eat breakfast, and your car is at my house anyway. Besides, Helen will throttle me if I show up without you."

Laughing at the image of the petite Helen strangling the much taller and stronger Cam, Mary nodded her head in agreement, "Alright Cam, I certainly don't be the one who is the cause of Helen being charged with GBH."

Waving goodbye as he left the lab, he couldn't help but smile at the thought of his wife causing grave bodily harm on anything except the beetles that had recently been attacking her beloved rose bushes.

Chapter 18

Bright and early Monday morning Sergeant Roberts stood knocking at the door of Alma Lacey's cottage at 61 Cottage Lane in Hereford. He had just raised his hand to knock again when the red door swung open, and Miss Lacey stood there with her purse draped over one arm, "I'm ready to go, Sergeant. Shall we get this show on the road, as the young people say?"

Dan smiled at the elderly lady as he held the front passenger door open for her, "Yes, Ma'am. Chief Inspector Fergus and the sketch artist will be meeting us at the station in Ross-on-Wye."

Settling into the seat and fastening her seatbelt, Miss Lacey reflected, "Ross-on-Wye...now that's a lovely market town. Wait, did you say, Chief Inspector Cam Fergus?"

"Yes ma'am, why?"

"I knew a Detective Cameron Fergus, but he was with the Met."

As he maneuvered through the crowded streets of Hereford, Dan glanced over at his passenger and tried to picture her in her former role with the Met, "Yes

117

ma'am that would be one and the same. The Chief Inspector took over here at the station about three years ago. He'll be glad to see an old workmate from London."

Smiling the older woman replied, "Oh Sergeant, I wouldn't be so sure of that. You might want to ask him what their nickname for me was."

The rest of the drive was made in relative silence as Miss Lacey peered out the window watching the scenery. It was obvious to Dan that the elderly lady didn't get out into the countryside often, and she was definitely enjoying the change of scenery.

Cam was just getting out of his car when Dan pulled his vehicle to a stop behind the station. Unconsciously straightening his tie, Cam strode over to the car and opened the door for Miss Lacey, "Detective Chief Inspector Lacey, it's good to see you again."

Stepping out of the car, the diminutive elderly woman pulled herself upright before taking her cane and poking Cam in the stomach, "Put on a few extra pounds there since we last met, and I see you still haven't learned to properly tie a tie."

With that, she stood on her toes and leaned forward and placed a kiss on Cam's cheek, much to Cam's surprise.

After escorting their visitor into the office and leaving her with the police artist in his office, Sergeant Roberts joined Cam in his office.

"Well, that certainly was a surprise. Old Iron Bottom must have mellowed in her old age," said Cam as he touched his cheek."

Dan started to laugh, "So that was what you called her. She said that she didn't think you would be glad to see her, and said her men had a nickname for her."

"You wouldn't know it by looking at her now, but she was the toughest boss I ever had. Everything had to be by the book, and if you stepped out of line, well, god help you."

By the time that Cam finished quickly checking his emails for anything urgent; he fixed a cup of tea for their visitor and headed for the Sergeant Roberts' office.

"I've brought you a cup of tea, Detective Chief Inspector."

"It's just plain Miss Lacey now, Chief Inspector or Alma if you can manage it," she said, turning her alert blue eyes on him.

Sitting down beside her as the artist worked on completing the sketch, Cam smiled back into the now warm and friendly eyes that had once caused fear to course through his veins, "I would be honored to call you Alma, as long as you call me Cam."

Reaching over and patting his hand, she replied, "Cam it is, then."

The warm reunion was abruptly interrupted when the police artist slid the sketch in front of Alma and Cam, "Is this a likeness of the man who you saw speaking to the victim."

"Yes, that's him."

Pushing the sketch closer to Alma, Cam said, "Please have a closer look. Are you 100% sure that this is the man you saw outside the coffee shop with the victim."

Pushing the sketch back, the elderly lady replied, "My vision is still perfect, and yes, that is the man I saw. I can tell by that look on your face that you recognize him. I hope he's not a friend of yours."

"No, he's not a friend of mine. More like a friend of a very dear friend of mine, I'm sorry to say," Cam replied, looking down at his watch. "How about you and I have some lunch before I drive you back home, Alma?"

Smiling brightly now, Cam's former boss replied, "That would be lovely; if you're sure you can spare the time."

"I just need to leave some instructions with Sergeant Roberts. He can manage everything from here. He's top-notch. Frankly, he's the best sergeant I've ever worked with. I'm surprised he hasn't moved onto bigger and better things," said Cam as he got up and went in search of Dan.

Cam found Dan waiting patiently in his office, "I have the background report on the Professor, Sir. Do you want to see it now?"

"Give me the highlights. I'm just leaving now to take Miss Lacey to lunch, before dropping her off at home, so I'll be a while."

"The report reveals that he had been married once over twenty years ago and later divorced his wife when she began an affair and deserted him. Apparently, the wife moved back to Ireland with her lover after emptying his bank account and running up considerable bills leaving his finances in a mess. He was forced to give up his home at a loss, and the records indicate that he had been living in rooms at the university for several years until he managed to pay off the debts."

"Any criminal record?"

Shaking his head, Dan Robert's said, "No sir, nothing, not even a traffic violation, and not a hint of scandal. Apparently, he is well-liked among faculty and students, a large number of which he mentors. From his background, he sure doesn't seem like someone who would murder two young girls."

Taking a deep sigh, Cam grabbed his car keys off the desk before turning back to Dan, "That may be true, but Miss Lacey has just positively identified the Professor as the last person to be seen speaking with Ali before she disappeared. Take a break for your lunch, and then swing by and bring the good Professor in for questioning. I shouldn't be very long."

Chapter 19

Cam selected a riverside pub as the lunch venue and was able to secure a table in the garden room, giving his former boss a view of the beautifully manicured lawns leading down to the fast-flowing River Wye.

"Will this do?" Cam asked as he held out a chair for Miss Lacey.

"This is just lovely, Cam. I'll bet it's even more beautiful in the spring when all the flowers are in bloom. Do you come here often?"

Pointing out the window, "Do you see that section of woodland to the left? Well, my wife, Helen, and I love to come here in May. The bluebells grow so thick in there that the trees appear to be floating on a carpet of blue. Add to that, the fact they serve a lovely Sunday roast, and you have a winning combination."

Rubbing her hands together like an excited child, "Sunday roast at the pub. How very lovely. None of the pubs near me serve a good roast dinner, anymore. They cater to the young university crowd, so it's all that fast food."

"Well, I tell you what, Alma. Helen and I have a reservation a week from Sunday. How would it be if I added one more person to that reservation and I pick you up."

"That would be wonderful, as long as your wife doesn't object."

"Helen will be happy to meet you. I've told her so much about you over the years."

Starting to laugh, the elderly lady said, "That's what I'm afraid of."

After a leisurely lunch of creamy leek soup, and cheddar and asparagus quiche, Cam dropped Alma. Lacey off at her cottage and reluctantly headed back to the station to question Professor Henderson. All the way back to Ross, Cam worried about how Mary was going to take the news that her first romantic interest, since the death of her husband years before, was possibly a murderer. He didn't have long to wait to find out.

Cam had just parked his car behind the station when he heard the unmistaken rattle of Mary's old Land Rover coming to a grinding halt.

"Hey Cam, Hereford sent me a new copy of the DNA test results from the scrapings I got from under Tony's nails. Unfortunately, there were no matches in the system."

Hesitating for a moment as her eyes lighted on the Professor's car, Mary asked, "What's Jim doing here, Cam."

"He's helping us with our inquiries, Mary. But before you go in there, I feel that you should know that he's been positively identified as the last person to be seen with Ali before she disappeared."

Mary's face seemed to lose most of its colour as she traced a circle in the gravel with her foot. After a brief moment, the professional in her took control of her emotions, "See if you can get a DNA sample from him, Cam. I'd like to get this resolved as soon as possible, for everyone's sake."

Putting his arm around her shoulders, Cam walked into the station with Mary. Leaving her in his office, Cam grabbed the evidence file and proceeded to the interview room where Sergeant Roberts sat quietly listening to the Professor discuss the latest finds from the dig at the castle.

Looking up as Cam entered the room, Henderson asked, "Chief Inspector, your Sergeant says that you have some more questions for me. I really don't know what else I can tell you."

"Well, Professor Henderson, you can start by telling us why you failed to mention that you had met the young woman who was unearthed in that trench at your dig."

Taken back by the question, the Professor started to stand up.

"Sit down, Professor," ordered Cam.

Slowly easing his lanky frame back into the chair, the Professor rested both his hands on the grey metal table and stared steadfastly into Cam's eyes, "I don't know what you're talking about, Chief Inspector!"

Pulling the photo of a smiling Ali from the evidence folder, Cam slid it across the table to the Professor, "Do you recognize this young lady, Professor."

Studying the photo for a few minutes, he scratched his head, and after a few minutes slowly replied, "Oh, dear Lord, is this the same girl that was in the trench?"

Cam carefully observed the expression on the man's face who sat opposite him. After all his years on the force, Cam had grown to be a good judge of human behavior. Judging from the Professor's reaction, he couldn't help but think, 'Either this man is a great actor, or he is genuinely shocked.'

"I'm sorry, Chief Inspector; I do remember this girl, now. It was nearly a month ago if I recall correctly. She was asking about her older sister and showed me a photo. I had seen her sister at one of the pubs closer to the university, and I directed her up there."

"Did you walk her there?"

"No, I had to get back to uni. I had a morning class that day, so we parted company at my turn-off to school."

"Did you ever see or speak with her after that, Professor?"

"Absolutely not, Chief Inspector, I can honestly say that I never saw her again after that day."

"OK Professor, there is one more thing, we'd like a sample for a DNA test so that we can exclude you from our inquiries. Will you have a problem with that?"

"Absolutely not, I have nothing to hide. I'm sorry that I failed to recognize the young lady. That poor child in the trench looked so different from the vibrant girl I met that day."

Sergeant Roberts, who had remained silent until then, readied the swab kit before blurting out, "Yeah, and the fact that someone had caved her skull in didn't help."

Cam rolled his eyes, "Thank you for your co-operation Professor. I'm afraid I'm going to have to ask you not to leave the area until otherwise advised. When is your dig due to wrap up, anyway?"

Putting his coat on and heading for the door, the Professor turned back, "We have four more days on the dig, and I am due back for classes the following Monday. Please let me know if it appears that you will need me for a longer period, so I can arrange for an associate to take my classes."

Rising to his feet to escort the Professor from the station, Cam said, "Hopefully, that won't be necessary, and this will be wrapped up by then. Thank you again for your co-operation."

As soon as Professor Henderson was out of sight, Cam turned to Sergeant Roberts, "Dan, We don't have enough to hold him, but I want him watched day and night. Can you arrange for that while I give this DNA sample to Mary?"

Cam leaned against the faded green wall outside the interview room, trying to decide on what bits of information he could share with Mary, based on her relationship with the suspect. Clutching the bag containing the DNA swab in his hand, Cam pushed open his office door to find Mary whispering on her mobile.

Holding a finger up, Mary signaled Cam to give her a moment. Finally, disconnecting from her call, she turned to Cam, "That was Jim. He saw my car parked out back and asked me to meet him for lunch. I put him off and told him that I'd phone him later. So, how did the interview go? Is he still a suspect?"

Cam held out the evidence bag containing the DNA sample, "That all depends on the results of this, but I feel it only fair to tell you that we will have to keep him under 24-hour surveillance until these murders are wrapped up. I am only telling you this Mary because I know that I can depend on your professional integrity not to disclose this to him."

Nodding, Mary replied, "You can rely on that, Cam."

Perching on the corner of the desk, Cam continued, "I showed him the photo of Ali, and he has admitted speaking with her but claims he only spoke to her the one time outside the coffee shop and never saw her again. He claims that he did not recognize the girl in the trench as the same girl he had briefly spoken with."

"I guess that much is possible, considering the amount of damage to the skull and the level of decomposition. What is your gut feeling, Cam? Did you believe him?"

Cam's forehead wrinkled up, "I'd rather reserve my opinion on that question, Mary. I have met some pathological liars during my career that could convince you that day is night, but if you must know...my gut feeling is...yes, I believe he was telling the truth."

"Thanks, Cam, that does make me feel a bit better. I'm going to personally deliver the sample to the lab in Hereford when I leave here. It can take 24-72 hours to get the results, but I'll push them, and hopefully, it will be closer to the lower end. Thank goodness that science has come a long way recently, or we'd be waiting weeks for this," said Mary as she walked down the hall with Cam and out into the brisk autumn day.

Cam placed a hand on Mary's arm, bringing her to a sudden stop, "Are you still planning on meeting your Professor tonight?"

When Mary pulled a face, he continued, "You're a grown woman and an intelligent one, but be careful. Make that meeting in a public place."

Nodding her agreement, Mary climbed up into her Land Rover and with a wave of her hand, was off on her way to Hereford.

Chapter 20

Mary had only just returned to her small-holding and was getting ready to tend to her animals when her mobile rang. Looking down at the number, she instantly recognized it as Jim's.

"Hello, Jim. No, I'm home, but I just got in and am getting ready to feed the animals.... Why, yes, that would be fine.... I'll meet you over at The Cove, say at 7:00 for dinner."

Jim Henderson hung up the phone and let out a sigh of relief. He had been afraid Mary would either not answer her phone when she recognized his number, or would just not agree to meet him for dinner, and he desperately wanted to explain his behavior after their last date. Time was going to drag until he got the chance.

Jim looked at his wristwatch for the third time in the ten minutes. Mary had promised to meet him at The Cove for dinner at 7:00, and it was now twenty minutes after. Shaking his head, he muttered to himself, "I can't say as I blame her."

He had just raised his hand to get the attention of the waiter, so he could get his bill for the glass of

Chablis he drank while waiting for Mary when the door opened and in she walked. Instead of apologizing for being late, Mary sat down and stared down at the table cloth with fists clenched in front of her before saying, "I've been sitting in the parking lot for the last twenty minutes, trying to make up my mind whether to come in or not."

Reaching over and laying his hand over Mary's clenched fist, Jim replied, "I'm so glad you decided to come in. I owe you an explanation."

Mary raised her eyes to meet Jim's, "Well, you better get on with it."

"First of all, Mary, I am so sorry about all the Champagne we drank the last time we were here. I was so interested in what we were talking about that I didn't realize that you had barely touched your meal. I also know that you suspect that I put something in your drink, but I swear to you that I would never do that to you or anyone."

Mary felt the heat of a blush moving up from her neck to her face, but before she could say anything, Jim held his hand up to silence her. "When I woke up the next morning, I realized that I handled the situation horribly and could have put you in grave danger. All I could think about was finding you and making sure you were okay. When I got to your house, and you weren't there, I was terrified that you could have gotten into your car when you shouldn't or gone outside and fallen. My mind was conjuring up awful images of you injured and alone, with no one to help you. I'm so sorry that I left you alone like that, Mary."

Leaning across the small table, Mary put a finger to Jim's lips to silence him, "I realize now that I misjudged you Jim, and for that, I'm very sorry."

"No, Mary, I should have stayed, I could have slept on the sofa, then I would have been there to keep an eye on you and explain that nothing out of line had transpired between us."

Shaking her head from side-to-side, "It was my fault for drinking too much, Jim. I was just so nervous about going on my first date since my husband died that I made a complete fool of myself."

Jim's lips turned up in a slight smile, "Yours too, huh? I hadn't been on a date since my wife walked out on me over twenty years ago."

Mary watched pain momentarily flash across Jim's face before it disappeared, and he regained his composure.

"I didn't know you had been married, Jim. For some reason, I always pictured you as a confirmed bachelor. Do you want to talk about it?"

"There's not much to tell. I married a former student, much younger than me, and maybe that was the problem, who knows? The long and short of it was I came home from work one day, and she was gone, along with everything of value in the flat. Talk about stupid, I even called the police and reported that my home had been burgled and my wife was missing. Can you imagine my embarrassment when the neighbors told the officers that they had witnessed my wife helping a young man load up my possessions and leaving together, arm-in-arm? Thank goodness, we never had children."

"Oh, Jim, I am so sorry. That is just horrible!"

"You don't know the half of it, Mary. She also emptied our bank account and maxed out my credit cards, so I was left with huge monthly bills and no cash to pay them. My credit was ruined, and I was forced to sell my flat and move back into apartments at the university. I guess that's probably why that I haven't had the desire to become too close to anyone since."

Just as Mary was opening her mouth to respond, their waiter approached the table, "Are you ready to order?"

Giving the menu another quick glance, Mary replied, "I think I'll have the trout tonight and a glass of sparkling water."

Directing his attention to Jim, he asked, "And you, sir?"

Handing the waiter his menu, Jim replied, "That sounds perfect. Make that two of the same."

Growing quiet for a moment, Mary gently said, "I had such a wonderful husband, and when I lost him, I knew that no one could ever take his place in my heart, so I never dated. I put all my energy into my little farm and my job. I do miss the companionship, just having someone to share a meal with or sit down to watch television with after a long day at work. I'm not looking to replace him. I hope you understand, Jim."

Letting out a huge sigh of relief, Jim again reached for Mary's hand, "Oh, thank you for being so honest, Mary. I feel the same way, not that I miss the ex-wife, heavens no, but I do miss having a good friend who I can go out with to a meal, someone who I can just pop in and visit when I'm in the area. I hope you can be that friend to me."

Chapter 21

Mary and Jim sat around Mary's kitchen table reminiscing about university days into the wee hours of the morning, causing her to get a late start to work. She had no sooner sat down at her desk before her phone began ringing. Holding the phone with one hand, while scrolling through her emails with the other, Mary answered the phone, "Mary Hamilton...Oh, hello, Cam....Sorry I was running a bit late this morning....Yes, I'm just checking to see if the results have come back from the lab....Can you hold on for a moment?"

Cam swiveled around in his chair and began doodling with his finger on the steamed-up windows. The room had grown stifling hot, and if the rain hadn't been thrashing down, he'd have thrown the window wide open. Cam's doodling on the steam covered window was abruptly interrupted by a sharp intake of breath on the other end of the phone line, "Cam, these results don't make sense at all. I really don't understand."

Cam's head tilted to the side, and he wiped his wet finger on his pants, "What don't you understand, Mary? What does the report say?"

Hesitating, Mary asked, "You remember that I was having dinner with Jim last night, don't you?"

Nodding his head and rising to his feet, Cam said, "It's him, then?"

"No! That's just it Cam, it's not Jim."

Pushing his hair back from his forehead, Cam dropped back in his chair, "Well, that's good, isn't it? But, what does the report have to do with you having dinner with the Professor last night?"

Still staring at the report, Mary said, "Jim or the Professor, as you insist upon calling him, told me that he was divorced and that his wife left him for another man."

Growing impatiently, Cam asked, "And what does that have to do with anything?"

"The DNA test reveals partial matches indicating that the murderer shares half his DNA with Jim. The murderer is Jim's son."

Hanging up the phone while Mary was still talking, Cam called to his sergeant, "Dan, the murderer is the Professor's son. Is PC Parks keeping him under surveillance today?

Dan quickly crossed the hall to Cam's office, "Yes, Sir, I just got off the phone with her."

"Good, call her back and tell her to bring the Professor in for further questioning. We need to find out where his son is hiding."

Realizing that Cam had hung up on her while she was trying to tell him that Jim told her that he had never had children, Mary grabbed her raincoat and headed out the door. She knew Cam was going to bring Jim in for more questioning. And she wanted some answers, too!

As she drove, Mary kept turning over a variety of scenarios in her head. Why had Jim lied to her about having a child? Had he known all along that his son committed these murders? Had he only renewed their friendship to try to get information out of her about the case?

The more questions that Mary asked herself, the more nothing made sense. If he knew that his son murdered these girls and buried them at the Castle, then why would he have organized a dig there? If it wasn't for the dig disturbing the bodies, they could have remained hidden for years with no one being the wiser. No...Nothing made sense.

Mary's old Land Rover had barely come to a stop when she jumped out of the car and headed for the station door where Cam stood waiting for the arrival of PC Parks and the Professor.

"What are you doing here, Mary?"

Shoving Cam aside as she barged through the door, Mary shouted, "For one thing, Cam Fergus, you hung up on me while I was still talking."

Cam was shocked; he had never heard Mary speak to anyone like this...especially, not him.

"Mary, I'm so sorry. I just wanted to get the Professor in here as quick as possible after what you told me about the DNA results."

Bristling, Mary sneered, "Well, if you hadn't hung up, you might have waited until you could do some further investigation."

Totally confused, Cam ushered Mary into his office, "Sit down and calm down Mary and tell me...investigate what? DNA doesn't lie, the Professor's son is the murderer, and he needs to tell us where he's hiding."

Growing silent for a moment, Mary finally replied, "I am sure Jim would be happy to cooperate if he could."

"Mary, you're losing me. What do you mean…if he could? Are you saying that he may not know where his son is?"

"Cam, I don't believe that Jim even knows that he has a son."

Leaning back in his chair, Cam let out a groan, "Perhaps, you better tell me why you think that this is possible."

Over the next ten minutes, Mary told Cam about her conversations with Jim during dinner the previous evening and the questions that had been swirling around in her head on the drive to the station. When she finished, Cam stood up and strode across the hall to his sergeant's office, "Dan, I want you to run a check on the name that appeared on the Professor's background report as his ex-wife. Run both her married and maiden name. I need it right away and when Anne gets here with the Professor, have her make him comfortable in the interview room, and don't mention anything about why we want to speak to him. Understood?"

"Yes, Sir, I'm on it."

Returning to his office, Cam poured Mary a cup of coffee and positioned himself at his desk so he could watch the parking lot while still speaking with Mary, "I trust your instincts, Mary, and I value your opinion. Dan is going to follow-up on the Professor's ex-wife, but that's still no guarantee that he didn't father a child by another woman, and just didn't want to share that information with you."

Nodding her agreement, "True, but if you could have heard the degree of disappointment in his voice at not having children, you might think differently."

Swiveling around in his chair at the sound of tyres on the gravel drive, Cam frowned, "He's here. For your sake, Mary, I hope you're right. I guess we'll know soon enough."

Chapter 22

Cam drummed his fingers on his desk as he watched the clock tick away the minutes. Professor Henderson had been waiting in the interview room for twenty minutes, and Cam was still waiting for Dan to complete running the background report on the Professor's ex-wife.

Jumping to his feet, Cam looked apologetically across at Mary, "I can't wait anymore. Obviously, Dan is having trouble getting the background report. I need to get in there."

Walking down the hall, Cam entered the interview room, sat down opposite the Professor, and switched on the recorder, "Interview commenced at 13:30, for the record Chief Inspector Cam Fergus and PC Anne Parks attending. PC Parks will you caution the prisoner?"

Stepping closer to the table, PC Parks addressed the Professor, "You do not have to say anything. But it may harm your defense if you fail to mention when questioned anything you later rely on in court. Do you understand?"

"This sounds serious, are you charging me with a crime?" asked the Professor.

Staring into the man's eyes, Cam responded, "That all depends on how co-operative you are. Now, do you understand your rights, Professor?"

"Yes, of course. I'll be glad to answer any questions you have for me, Chief Inspector."

Leaning across the table and carefully watching the Professor's face, Cam was just about to ask him where his son was hiding when a knock on the door, followed by Dan sticking his head in, and motioning for Cam to join him and Mary in the hallway, interrupted the interview.

"Sir, it appears that the Professor's ex-wife did have a child. The boy was born eight months after she left the marital home."

"So, it's a possibility that the Professor wouldn't be aware that he has a son if the wife chose to keep it a secret. We'll need to talk to her, Dan."

Shaking his head, Dan continued, "That's what took me so long. I'm afraid that won't be possible. The lady is deceased. That was how I discovered the son. It seems that she was living in Ireland under her

146

maiden name when struck by a car and killed. According to the records, her son claimed the body."

"Good work, Dan. What's the son's name, and do we have an address?"

"Michael Jameson and his address was listed as Hereford University."

Cam placed his hand on the doorknob to re-enter the interview room when Mary grabbed him by the sleeve, "Go easy on him, Cam. If I'm right, Jim has no idea his wife was pregnant when she left. In all reality, she probably didn't either, either she didn't know it was her husbands or she did and tried to pass the child off as her lovers. I guess we will never know."

Turning back and taking a deep breath as he placed his hand on the doorknob again, Cam slowly opened the door and entered.

Switching the recorder back on, Cam stared into the Professor's eyes, "Professor Henderson, we need to speak to your son. Do you know where he is hiding?"

The Professor's reaction was far from what Cam expected. Once the look of utter bewilderment left the man's eyes, he slowly replied, "There must be some mistake, Chief Inspector. I don't have a son. I have never been fortunate enough to be blessed with children."

"Professor, I understand that your wife left you for another man. Is that correct?"

"Why yes, that's true, Chief Inspector. I expect Mary told you that. I came home one day, and she was gone."

Peering down at the papers that Dan had given him and not wanting to violate Mary's confidence, "Actually, no. It's right here in your application for a divorce. The DNA test revealed that the man who we suspect murdered three people shares fifty percent of your DNA. I'm sure you know what that means, Professor. We traced your ex-wife, and I am sorry to tell you that she died as a result of a motor vehicle accident and that her body was claimed by her son...your son. "

Professor Henderson held up a shaking hand, "I had no idea that she was pregnant when she left. I never heard from her after she disappeared."

"Apparently, she was married briefly and the son... your son... was named after him."

"I'm having a hard time taking all this in, Chief Inspector, but if I didn't know I even had a son, then how can I help you?"

Looking down at the papers before staring back into Henderson's eyes, "Do you know a Michael Jameson? Our information indicates he lives at Hereford University, quite a coincidence if you ask me."

Reaching for his glass of water, his hand jerked, and water flooded the desk as he jumped to his feet, "Michael Jameson? Are you saying that he's my son?"

"Yes, are you saying that he never gave any indication that you were his father?"

"Good lord, no! I mentored him, and he works with me. He's the Associate Professor working with me at the dig. As a matter of fact, Michael is the one that recommended the site and did all the background research before we came down here. He's the one that chose the area for his team to dig, and he's the one that alerted me to the bodies. Are you sure he's the murderer, Chief Inspector?"

"I'm afraid so, DNA matching his was found under the fingernails of Tony Lambert and also on the jacket he wore the night he was pushed off the walls of

149

Goodrich Castle. We will need a DNA sample from Mr. Jameson to be 100% sure, but as long as you're certain that your late ex-wife is the only one who could have born you a child, then I think that is little choice, but to arrest him."

Wringing his hands, "No, she was the only one. I just can't believe that I've been this close to my own son for years and had no idea. He never gave me any indication. Is it possible that this is all a series of coincidences, and he doesn't know that I'm his father?"

"I find that highly unlikely, Professor. Where is Mr. Jameson now?"

"I left him in charge at the dig, when your officer asked me to accompany her here."

Cam pushed up from the table, "We need to get there right away!"

"He's my son, Chief Inspector, can I come with you? Perhaps, if he sees you bringing me back, then he won't be alarmed and attempt anything foolish."

Grabbing his coat, he nodded at the Professor and called to Sergeant Roberts, "We need to get up to the dig. The Professor is riding with us. I want it to look like we are just driving him back. We don't want to tip-off our suspect."

Mary stood silently in the hall, waiting for her friend to come out of the interview room. Grabbing his arm as he walked into the hall, "Jim, I know this has all come as quite a shock to you, and believe me when I say, I am so terribly sorry. Please call me if there is anything I can do?"

Placing his hand over hers, Professor Henderson gazed into Mary's troubled eyes and squeezed her hand before nodding, then followed Cam and Sergeant Roberts out of the station.

As the three men pulled out of the station lot, Cam called Hereford for backup, "The murder suspect is Assistant Professor Michael Jameson. He is currently in charge of the archeological dig at Goodrich Castle. We are on the way there and will wait out of sight until backup arrives. Under no circumstances are you to use sirens or approach the suspect. He has at least a dozen students with him, and we definitely don't want to risk a hostage situation."

Reaching over the back seat, and placing his hand on Cam's shoulder, Professor Henderson said, "Chief Inspector, I've had a thought. Perhaps if you drop me off at the welcome centre and appear to leave, I could return to the dig as if nothing happened. I realize that you say that Jameson is my son, but my main concern is for the safety of my students. I would prefer to get him separated from the group before you move in."

Turning around in his seat to face the man, Cam replied, "That's a good idea. How do you plan on getting him away from them?"

"I'll go back and carry on, as usual, then I'll go up on the castle walls and call Jameson to come up and look at something unusual that I've noticed in the topography of the trench. Once he's up there with me, I'll put my hand up to my eyes like I am shading them from the sun, and then point down to the trench. That will be your signal to have your men move-in."

Cam looked over to his Sergeant checking his reaction before replying, "If you're sure you can carry it off Professor, it's worth a try. We need him separated from the group before we attempt an arrest."

The rain had finally let up as they pulled into the Welcome Centre parking area to find Jameson and the rest of the team exited the building from a break. Cam looked back at the man in the backseat, "Follow my lead, Professor. If he asks, tell him we've brought in

Charlie Hopwood and are in the process of charging him, and we needed you to identify him as the man you saw with Ali at the coffee shop."

As Cam climbed out of the front seat and opened the back door for Professor Henderson to exit the car, Michael Jameson approached the vehicle. Reaching his hand out and firmly grasping the Professor's outstretched hand, Cam smiled and shaking his hand, loudly thanked him, "Thank you for coming in and helping us with our inquiries, Professor. Looks like this case will be wrapped up very quickly now, and we won't have to disturb your work here again."

As Cam climbed back into the front passenger seat and waved goodbye before driving away, Professor Henderson walked over to stand beside young Jameson.

"Is everything alright, Professor?" asked the gaunt-faced, young man.

"Yes, it looks like that young man who I saw talking to the victim at the coffee shop has been charged with her murder. What in the world would make someone take another person's life? Such a terrible waste."

As they walked back towards the dig, Professor Henderson glanced sideways at the young man, who he now knew to be his son, to see if he could glimpse any sign of remorse on his face. There was none. He knew now that he had no choice.

Chapter 23

The team was busy working in the moats by the time the estranged father and son returned to the site. As soon as Michael climbed down the ladder into the moat to join his group of students, the Professor made his way across the bridge over the moat and slowly made his way up the narrow stone stairway. As he climbed up, the Professor felt the weight of the world on his shoulders as he thought of all the years he had missed when his son was growing up. He couldn't help but wonder if he had known about his existence and shared in raising him if things would have turned out differently. Shaking his head, Henderson realized that all the "what-ifs" in the world wouldn't change today's outcome. Today, the son he'd never known was going to be arrested and charged with three counts of murder, and there was nothing he could do to change this.

Back on the exit road, hidden out of sight, Cam was dispensing his men in the woods surrounding the castle and the fields beyond. As soon as Professor Henderson gave the signal, they would move in.

Crouching behind a tree, Sergeant Roberts broke the uneasy silence, "Do you think the Professor can pull it off, Sir."

"I hope so, but right now our main concern is getting any potential hostages clear of the area. There have already been too many lives lost."

Professor Henderson stared down at the mote below him where Jameson stood smiling and easily chatting with the students on his team. He still couldn't wrap his head around the fact that this soft-spoken young man could have murdered these girls, and then pushed that young man to his death off this very castle wall. Feeling the wind on his face as the sky darkened and a cloud covered the sun, the Professor cupped his hands to his mouth and called out, "Jameson, come up here and have a look at this. I think I've discovered something."

Turning and looking up, the young man smiled and waved back, "I'll be right up, Professor."

Professor Henderson waited until Jameson joined him on the outer wall before shielding his eyes and pointing down towards the moat, giving Cam the signal he was waiting for. Within minutes, police were swarming the area rounding up the students and moving them out of harms- way. It was only then that Cam approached the castle and called out, "Michael Jameson, I'm Chief Inspector Fergus with West Mercia Police, the area is surrounded. We'll need you to come down and come with us."

The young man's eyes grew wide as he looked around for any possible avenue of escape. There was none, and he knew in an instant that was precisely why he had been drawn up to the castle wall.

Turning on the Professor, he sneered, "You did this to me. You set me up."

Reaching out a hand and placing it on Jameson's arm, the older man, tears streaming down his cheeks, could only reply, "I'm so sorry, son. It's over. It's time to go down."

Slapping the Professor's hand away, "So, you know, do you? I couldn't believe that all these years we worked together so closely, and you never figured it out. Even with all the hints, I dropped. I guess Mother was right about you being book smart because you sure do suck at real life. You don't have a clue what it was like for me growing up...the beatings from my drunken mother, the abuse from every man she took up with and believe me, there were a lot of them, and the bullying at school."

Perhaps it was just the cloak of mist that had suddenly shrouded the castle, or perhaps it was his mind playing tricks on him, but as he stared into the terrified eyes of his trapped son, he saw the image of a young child cowering in the corner. Perhaps that's what made him step forward to try to comfort him and attempt to embrace the son he could no longer shelter and protect. Whatever it was, we will never know.

As the grieving father stepped forward, Michael suddenly turned away, and the older man lost his balance on the wet stones. The next few seconds seemed a lifetime as Cam stood watching and helpless to do anything to stop the inevitable, as the Professor's body landed with a sickening thud on the castle floor below. After a few seconds of silence, the only sound that could be heard through the mist was the anguished cry of "Father' from the castle wall.

As Sergeant Roberts called for Emergency Services, Cam raced across the wooden, timber bridge over the moat into the castle. When he reached the spot where the twisted body of the Professor lay, he found Michael Jameson gently cradling his father's head in his lap as he softly talked to him and tried desperately to wipe away the blood still streaming from his father's face. Slowly approaching, Cam squatted beside the Professor's still body and placed his fingertips to his neck, hoping to feel any evidence of a pulse. There was none.

At the sound of his sergeant's footsteps racing toward the horrific scene, Cam held up his hand to stop him, "Give him a few minutes with his father." At that very moment, Cam saw the young man through the eyes of his grieving father. He no longer saw a vicious murderer but a lost, little boy grieving for the father that he had never really known and now...never would.

When Michael Jameson was led away to the waiting police cars, the hunted murderer had vanished, never to return, and in his place was a shy, abused child crying for his father.

Epilogue

"What will happen to him now?" asked Mary as she sat in Cam and Helen's kitchen two weeks later.

Mary had been very quiet during the first dinner that she shared with her friends since Professor Henderson's funeral. It had been a big affair attended by hundreds, as the entire faculty and hordes of students came out to pay their respects. It amazed Mary that Jim could have been so lonely while surrounded by people that obviously respected and cared for him, but in so many ways he was.

Between mouthfuls of roast lamb, Cam replied, "Well, the preliminary reports have come in from the psychiatrists, and as long as the rest of the tests concur with their findings, the Professor's son will never come to trial."

Mary nodded, "What will become of him?"

"He will in all likelihood be confined to a secure psychiatric facility for the rest of his life or until they are sure, beyond a shadow of a doubt, that he's no longer a threat to himself or anyone else. To be honest with you, Mary, I will be stunned if that ever occurs."

Helen had remained silent, determined not to say anything to further upset her dear friend, but finally said, "I suppose that will be some consolation for the victim's families."

Mary nodded again, and this time as she spoke, her hands began to shake, "I spoke with the parents of the two sisters when their remains were finally released. Did you know that the father is actually a psychiatrist himself? Of course, he has been following the case, and he said that he and his wife were hoping that Jim's son would not go to prison but to a mental hospital."

Helen reached across the table for her friend's hand, "I guess, we will never know why he killed the girls, or why he set up a dig at the castle and led his team to exactly the spot he had buried them."

"I can't answer why he committed the murders, but I think that he buried Ali with her sister during a period of remorse, and then chose the location for the dig during a brief window of sanity. I honestly believe that he felt himself slipping farther and farther into insanity and wanted the bodies found."

What Mary said next stunned both Helen and Cam, "Do you think the officials at the institution will allow me to visit Jim's son?'

Cam's brow furrowed as he asked, "Do you think that's wise, Mary? Do you really want to do that?"

Gazing across the table at Cam, Mary replied, "If Jim had lived, I have no doubt that he would have visited him. It's the least I can do for my old friend."

Cam had his doubts about the prudence of the planned visits, but all concerns were lifted as Christmas approached, and Mary seemed to have shaken off the depression that had plagued her since her friend's untimely death. In her free time, Mary volunteered at the hospital where she was known as the "animal lady" for bringing every imaginable breed of livestock to visit the patients confined there. She could often be seen walking the grounds and talking with her friend's son.

As for Michael Jameson, the doctors at the institution diagnosed him with having the mind of a nine-year-old child, brought on most likely by childhood abuse and the trauma of his father's death. Michael exhibited no awareness of the brutal murders he had committed or the tragic death of his father. He remained a shy, timid child trapped in the body of a grown man, but with medication and treatment, he was finally happy now, and no longer the frightened, abused child of his youth.